THE CONQUERORS

THE CONQUERORS

ANDRÉ MALRAUX

TRANSLATED BY STEPHEN BECKER

HOLT, RINEHART AND WINSTON
NEW YORK

Library of Congress Cataloging in Publication Data
Malraux, André, 1901–
The conquerors.

Translation of Les conquérants.
1. China—History—1912–1937—Fiction. I. Title.
PZ3.M2989Co12   [PQ2625.A716]   843′.9′12   72-91594
ISBN 0-03-007716-8

Originally published in French under the title
Les Conquérants

Designer: Madelaine Caldiero
PRINTED IN THE UNITED STATES OF AMERICA
10 9 8 7 6 5 4 3 2 1

To the memory of my friend René Latouche

PART ONE

THE APPROACHES

A GENERAL STRIKE HAS BEEN CALLED IN CANTON.

The bulletin has been posted since yesterday, underlined in red.

As far as the horizon, the Indian Ocean lies glassy, lacquered, not a ripple. A cloudy sky presses down like the fug in a bathhouse, wraps us in humid air. The passengers pace the deck methodically, careful not to wander too far from the white-framed board where bulletins monitored tonight will be tacked up. Every day, reports sharpen the outlines of the dawning drama; it takes shape; finally a direct threat, it haunts every man on this steamer. Until now the Cantonese government has waged a war of words: and here suddenly the telegrams translate action. What troubles everybody is not so much the riots, strikes, and streetfighting as the unexpected resolve, apparently as stubborn as England's pride, not to settle for talk anymore, but to strike at what matters most to England: her wealth and her prestige. The ban on the sale of all English merchandise in provinces controlled by the Cantonese government, even if offered by Chinese merchants; the systematic supervision of the markets, one after another; sabotage of machinery by workers in Hong Kong; and finally this general strike attacking the whole business life of the British island, while newspaper correspondents report unusual activity in the Cantonese military academies—all that puts these passengers up against a new kind of war, launched by the anarchic power of South China supported by allies

[3]

they know almost nothing about, against the very symbol of British dominion in Asia, the military rock from which the armed Empire watches over its flocks: Hong Kong.

Hong Kong. The island is there on the map, black, sharply outlined, like a bolt closing off the Pearl River. The river is lined on both banks by the gray mass of Canton, with stippling to mark the irregular suburbs only a few hours from the British cannon. Every day passengers stare at the small black spot as if awaiting some revelation, at first worried, now sullen, fretfully conjecturing how this place that their lives depend on will defend itself—this richest mass of rock in the world.

If it's attacked, sooner or later reduced to the rank of a minor port, or even if it simply weakens, then China will be able to rally the cadres that she's so far lacked, to fight the white man, and European dominance will collapse. The cotton and bristle traders among my fellow passengers feel that acutely, and it's startling to read on their anguished faces (*but what will become of the Company?*) a reflection of the tremendous struggle initiated by the very empire of chaos, suddenly organized, against the one nation that stands more than any other for will, tenacity, strength.

A great bustle on deck. The passengers rush, jostle, squeeeze close: here come the printed bulletins.

SWITZERLAND, GERMANY, CZECHOSLOVAKIA, AUSTRIA, never mind, never mind. RUSSIA, let's see that. No, nothing important. CHINA, ah!

MUKDEN: CHANG TSO-LIN . . .

Never mind.

CANTON.

The outermost passengers, pressing closer, squeeze us against the bulkhead.

LED BY RUSSIAN OFFICERS, THE CADETS OF THE WHAMPOA MILITARY ACADEMY, THE VANGUARD OF A HUGE HOST OF

STUDENTS AND WORKERS, HAVE OPENED FIRE ON SHAMEEN.*
EUROPEAN SAILORS DETAILED TO PROTECT THE BRIDGES HAVE
RETURNED FIRE WITH MACHINE GUNS. THE CADETS, SPURRED
ON BY RUSSIAN OFFICERS, HAVE LAUNCHED SEVERAL ASSAULTS
ON THE BRIDGES. THEY HAVE BEEN REPULSED WITH HEAVY
LOSSES.

THE WIVES AND CHILDREN OF EUROPEANS IN SHAMEEN
WILL BE EVACUATED TO HONG KONG, IF POSSIBLE, ABOARD
AMERICAN SHIPS. THE WITHDRAWAL OF BRITISH TROOPS IS
IMMINENT.

Silence falls abruptly.

The passengers scatter in consternation. Meanwhile to
my right two Frenchmen meet: "One wonders, Monsieur,
one really wonders when the governments will make up
their minds to adopt the vigorous attitude that . . ." and
turn their steps to the bar, the end of the sentence lost in
the muffled jolting of the engines.

We're still ten days from Hong Kong.

5 P.M.

SHAMEEN. THE ELECTRICITY IS OUT. THE ENTIRE CONCES-
SION IS BLACKED OUT. THE BRIDGES HAVE BEEN HASTILY
FORTIFIED AND BARRICADED WITH BARBED WIRE. THEY ARE
ILLUMINATED BY GUNBOATS' SEARCHLIGHTS.

29 JUNE
SAIGON

A dreary, deserted provincial city, with long avenues and
straight boulevards where grass grows beneath lush tropical trees. My ricksha man is sweating: it's a long trip.
Finally we come to a Chinese neighborhood, full of small
banks, all sorts of offices, and gilt signs with beautiful

* European concession in Canton.

[5]

black characters. In front of me, down the middle of a wide, grassy avenue, a little trolley car frisks. Number 37, 35, 33 . . . stop! We've halted at a house like all the others in this neighborhood. Some sort of office. The plaques of obscure Cantonese business firms line both sides of the doorway. Inside, behind dusty, sagging counters, two Chinese employees are dozing: one cadaverous, dressed in white, the other obese, the color of baked clay, naked to the waist. On the wall, color pictures of Shanghai: girls with meticulously barbered bangs, monsters, landscapes. Just in front of me, three bicycles in a tangled heap. I am in the office of the president of the Kuomintang of Cochin China. In Cantonese I ask, "Is the boss in?"

"Not back yet, Monsieur. But go on up and make yourself at home."

I go up to the second floor by a kind of ladder. Nobody here. I sit. With nothing to do, I look around. A European armoire, a marble-topped Louis Philippe table, a Chinese settee of black wood, a splendid American armchair bristling with handles and screws. In the mirror above me, a large portrait of Sun Yat-sen and a photograph, smaller, of the master of this house. With a sizzling sound and the click of a soup vendor's metal cricket, the strong smell of Chinese fats cooking rises through the window. . . .

The clack of clogs.

In walk the proprietor, two other Chinese, and a Frenchman, Gérard, the one I'm here to see. Introductions. They press green tea upon me, and they instruct me to assure the Central Committee "that every party chapter in French Indochina is faithful to the democratic institutions which" et cetera.

Finally Gérard and I leave. Special envoy of the Kuomintang in Indochina, he's been here only a few days. He's a small man with a graying mustache and beard, and he looks like Czar Nicholas II, with the same uneasy, timid expression and the same obvious benevolence. There is something in him of the nearsighted professor, of the country doctor; he shuffles along beside me, preceded by a cigarette stuck into the end of a long, slim holder.

His car is waiting for us at the corner. We settle in and drive off slowly through the countryside. The rush of air creates a new climate: weary and tense at the same time, the muscles relax.

"What's new?"

"What you already know from the newspapers. The timing of strike orders from the various workers' committees seems to have been perfect. And so far the English don't know how to handle it: the merchant militia is a joke, good enough for one riot, maybe, but not for a strike. The ban on rice exports guarantees Hong Kong food for a while, but we never even dreamed of starving the city; what for? The rich Chinese backing the counterrevolutionary groups are dazed by the ban; it's as if somebody'd clubbed them."

"But since yesterday?"

"Nothing."

"You think the Cochin Chinese government is holding back the dispatches?"

"No. The personnel in the wireless office are almost all Young Annam; we'd have been warned. It's Hong Kong not transmitting."

A pause.

"And your Chinese sources?"

"The Chinese sources follow the propaganda line and that's all you can say for them. They say certain chambers of commerce have asked their president to declare war on England, they say English soldiers in Shameen have been taken prisoner by the Cantonese, they say prodigious demonstrations are in the works. Nonsense! What's serious, what's sure, is that for the first time ever the British in

Hong Kong are watching money slip away. The boycott was good. The strike is better. And what comes after the strike? Too bad we don't know what's happening. I ought to be hearing something any minute. Anyway, for two days no ship has cast off for Hong Kong. They're all there, up the river."

"And here?"

"We're doing pretty well, you know; you'll be able to leave with at least six thousand dollars. I'm waiting for another six hundred but I can't be sure. And I've only been here four days."

"They're pretty well fired up, if results mean anything."

"Oh, all the way! Enthusiasm is fairly rare among the Chinese, but this time they're excited, no question. And when you think that almost the whole six thousand comes from poor people: coolies, dockers, artisans . . ."

"Well, they have good reason to be hopeful. Outbreaks in Hong Kong, Shameen . . ."

"Oh sure, this sneaky war against an immobilized England, paralyzed—England!—is intoxicating. But all that's not very Chinese."

"Are you so sure?"

He falls silent, wedged in a corner of the car, eyes half shut, either thinking or relaxing, bathing himself in the cool air that washes away our fatigue. In the shifting blue of dusk, rice paddies flit along beside us, great gray mirrors painted here and there, in a blurred wash, with shrubs and pagodas, and the tall pylons of the wireless station towering above them. Compressing his lips and chewing on his mustache, he answers: "Do you know about the Monad plot that the British just uncovered in Hong Kong?"

"I don't know anything. I just got here."

"All right then. A secret society, the Monad, notices that travel between Hong Kong and Canton has been reduced to one little steamboat, the *Honan*. When this steamer's in port in Hong Kong, she's guarded by a British officer and a detail of sailors. The members of this society realize, very sensibly, the advantage there may be in preventing that boat from sailing for Canton with British arms for the counterrevolutionaries."

"None of our men on the steamer?"

"No. And the arms are off-loaded to fishing boats at some lonely spot in the Pearl River. It's like smuggling hash in the Suez Canal.

"Back to the plot: six members, acutely aware that they're risking their necks, kill the officer and the sailors, take over the ship, work aboard her for four hours and are caught at dawn by a British volunteer patrol just as they go ashore, making off with—care to guess?—one of the two twenty-foot stem posts that the Chinese paint the boat's eyes on."

"I don't think I understand."

"Those eyes help the boat to steer. One-eyed, she'll run aground."

"Oh. Oh!"

"That surprises you? Well, by God, me too. But the point is, here's your most serious group, the one you have most confidence in, and when the time comes they're ready to drop everything to go steal an eye painted on a piece of wood." And seeing my smile: "You think I'm generalizing, exaggerating. Well, you'll see. Things like that. Borodin and Garine will give you a hundred examples."

"Do you know Garine well?"

"Well, we've worked together. What do you want me to tell you? Do you know how he operates as head of Propaganda?"

"Just barely."

"Ah! It's . . . No. Hard to explain. You know that China was never used to philosophies of action, and they took hold of her the way equality took hold of Frenchmen in 1789.

[9]

Unresisting victims. Maybe it was like that all through yellow Asia: in Japan, when German lecturers began to preach Nietzsche, inspired students flung themselves off cliffs. It's more mysterious in Canton, and maybe even scarier. The simplest notion of the individual was unknown. Coolies are learning that they exist, just that they exist. . . . There's a popular ideology, like a popular art, that isn't just vulgarization, but *something else*. Borodin's propaganda said to the workers and peasants, 'You're terrific people because you're workers, because you're peasants, and because you belong to the two greatest forces of the State.' That didn't go over at all. They figured the way you recognized the two greatest forces of the State was, they were being bludgeoned and dying of hunger. They were too used to being despised because they were workers, or peasants. They were afraid that when the revolution was over, they'd be plunged right back into the contempt they were trying to liberate themselves from.

"Nationalist propaganda, Garine's, didn't tell them anything like that. But it got under their skin and worked them up violently—and unexpectedly—by making it possible for them to believe in their own dignity, their own importance, if you like. You have to see a dozen ricksha boys, with those faces like sly cats, their rags, and their wicker hats, do the manual of arms as a militia, surrounded by a respectful crowd, to suspect what we've done. The French and Russian revolutions were powerful because they gave every man his own share of the world; but this revolution is giving every man his own life. And no Western power can stop that.

"Hate! They keep trying to explain it all by hate! How simple! Our volunteers are fanatics for a lot of reasons, but mainly because now they've had a glimpse of another life, and after that all you can do with the old one is spit on it! Maybe so far Borodin hasn't understood that too well."

"Do they get along, these two Great White Fathers?"

"Borodin and Garine?"

At first I have the feeling that he doesn't want to answer. But no; he's thinking it over, his face lean and intent. Dusk deepens slowly. Over the sound of our motor all we can hear is the rhythmic rasping of cicadas. Still the rice paddies flit by on both sides of the road; on the horizon a palm tree shifts slowly.

"I don't think," he goes on, "that they get along *well*. They get along, that's all. They complement each other. Borodin is a man of action, Garine . . ."

"Garine?"

"Is a man capable of action. When the opportunity offers. Listen, you're going to find two kinds of men in Canton. First, the ones who came along in Sun's time, 1921, 1922, to take their chances or stake their lives, and who have to be called adventurers; for them China's a great pageant that they play parts in. Revolutionary fervor does for these men what a taste for army life does for members of the French Foreign Legion—they're men who've never been able to conform in ordinary society, who've asked a great deal of life, who wanted to give some meaning to their own lives, and who now, coming out the other side of all that, *serve*. And second, those who came with Borodin, professional revolutionaries for whom China is raw material. You'll find the first bunch in Propaganda, and almost all the second bunch in the labor movement and the army. Garine represents—and directs—the first bunch, who have less power but a lot more intelligence."

"Were you in Canton before Borodin?"

"Yes," he says, smiling, "but believe me, I'm talking objectively."

"And before that?"

He's silent. Is he going to tell me it's none of my business? He wouldn't be wrong. . . . No. He's still smiling.

And setting his hand lightly on my knee: "Before, I was a high school teacher in Hanoi." His smile grows broader, more ironic too, and his hand presses. "But I preferred something else, you see." He goes on quickly, as if to keep me from asking more questions: "Borodin is a big business-man. Hardworking, brave, daring when he has to be, very simple, wrapped up in his work."

"A big businessman?"

"A man compelled to ask about each thing, 'Can this be useful to me, and how?' That's Borodin. All his generation of Bolsheviks were scarred by their struggle with the anarchists; they all think that the main thing is to grapple with reality, with the difficulties of the exercise of power. And the memory of his own adolescence is vivid—a young Jew busy reading Marx in a tiny Latvian village, contempt all around him and Siberia a real possibility. Ah, cicadas, cicadas."

"When do you expect to have the news you mentioned?"

"In a few minutes. We're going to have dinner with the president of the Cholon chapter.* He runs a restaurant-opium parlor like that one."

Yes: now we're passing restaurants decorated with mirrors and enormous Chinese characters, in an atmosphere where life is all lights and noises; masses of glinting re-flectors, windows, lamps, and naked bulbs, the sounds of mah-jongg, phonographs, singing voices, shrill flutes, cymbals, gongs. . . .

Now the lights are massed thicker. The driver shifts gears and fidgets, leaning on the horn constantly to make his way through a crowd of white cloth denser than the crowds on European boulevards: workers, poor Chinese of all trades, strolling as they nibble at sweets and fruits,

* Cholon is the Chinese quarter of Saigon; large, rich, important. (Tr.)

[1 2]

hardly budging to make room for the cars that squeal and grind while the Annamite drivers shout insults. Here nothing is French anymore.

The car stops in front of a restaurant–opium parlor not fronted by ugly iron balconies like most we've seen, but less colonial, more like a small town house. As usual the entrance, beneath two Chinese characters in black on a gold ground, is all mirrors, to the left, to the right, to the rear, and even on the stairway risers. In the cashier's window a fat Chinese naked to the waist—it's all we can see of him—is toting up his accounts on an abacus, half blocking our view of a long room where, in the shadows, orange-tinted bodies and agile hands are busy about an immense platter of pearly crayfish and a pyramid of delicate scarlet empty shells.

On the second floor a Chinese in his forties with a bulldog face welcomes us (introductions) and ushers us immediately into a private room where three of his compatriots are waiting. Spotless white suits, prussian collars. On the black wooden settee, pith helmets. Introductions. (Impossible to hear any of the names, of course.) A small table without a cloth, covered with dishes and small cups full of sauces; wicker armchairs. The glow of many bulbs hung from the ceiling brightens the busy night. A din constantly exaggerated by salvos of firecrackers, the click-clack of dominoes, the belling of gongs and, now and then, the meowing of a single-stringed fiddle, invades the room on gusts of warm air that the fans strain to scatter.

The bulldog, who is proprietor and interpreter, tells me, under his breath and with a strong accent: "Monsieur the Director of the French Hospital, he came to dine here this week." He seems very proud of it, but is interrupted by the oldest of his friends: "Tell them that——"

Gérard informs them immediately that I understand Cantonese; their fellow feeling wells, and conversation begins: democratic chitchat, "the rights of the people," et cetera. I have the very strong impression that these men's only strength springs from a sense of outrage, that the evils they've suffered are the only thing they're really aware of. They remind me of the provincial societies under the Convention after the French Revolution (but these Chinese are men of exquisite courtesy, which contrasts oddly with their habit of swabbing the sweat off their necks). How much faith they all have in words! And how ineffectual they must feel by contrast with the operating groups they finance!

Here's what they've learned today, all jumbled together:

IN ALL THE CITIES OF THE INTERIOR THE BRITISH ARE FLEEING TO THE INTERNATIONAL CONCESSIONS.

THE LARGE COOLIE FEDERATIONS HAVE DECIDED THAT FROM NOW ON EACH MEMBER WILL CONTRIBUTE FIVE CENTS A DAY IN AID OF THE HONG KONG STRIKERS.

TREMENDOUS DEMONSTRATIONS ARE BEING PREPARED IN SHANGHAI AND PEKING TO COMMEMORATE THE UNJUST VIOLENCE INFLICTED BY FOREIGN IMPERIALISM AND TO AFFIRM CHINESE FREEDOM.

MASSES OF VOLUNTEERS ARE ENLISTING IN THE SOUTHERN PROVINCES.

THE CANTONESE ARMY HAS JUST RECEIVED A CONSIDERABLE QUANTITY OF WAR MATÉRIEL FROM RUSSIA.

And then this, shrewdly printed in large characters:

A CUTOFF OF ELECTRICITY IN HONG KONG IS IMMINENT.

FIVE TERRORIST ATTACKS TOOK PLACE YESTERDAY. THE CHIEF OF POLICE IS GRAVELY WOUNDED.

THE CITY IS ABOUT TO RUN OUT OF WATER.

And finally news of international politics, almost all of it about a certain Ch'eng-tai.

Dinner over, Gérard and I go downstairs, in a flurry of white sleeves and sweeping bows, and decide to walk for a bit. The air is cool. On the river not far off, in a bellow carried a long way on the humid air, an occasional steamboat whistle rises above the din of Chinese restaurants.

Gérard walks along to my right, fidgety. He blotted up a fair amount of wine this evening.

"You feeling poorly?"

"No."

"You seem upset."

"Yes." As he answers he realizes that his tone is too sharp, and he adds quickly, "There's reason enough."

"But everybody seemed delighted."

"Oh, them!"

"And the news is good."

"What news?"

"What they just told us, for God's sake! The power blackout, the——"

"Then you didn't hear what the fellow next to me was saying?"

"Fellow next to *me* was talking about his father and the revolution. The least I could do was pay attention."

"He said Ch'eng-tai's going to come out openly against us."

"So?"

"What do you mean, so? Isn't that enough?"

"It might be enough if I——"

"Let's just say he's the most influential man in Canton."

"In what way, influential?"

"I can't explain, exactly. Don't worry, you'll hear plenty about him. He's the spiritual head of the party's right wing. His friends call him the Chinese Gandhi. True, they're wrong."

"Be specific: what does he want?"

"Be specific! You're young, all right. . . . I don't really know. Maybe he doesn't either."

"But why does it bother you?"

[15]

"Our relations were fairly strained. Now it looks as if he's about to denounce us to the Committee of Seven and world opinion."

"For what?"

"How do I know? Ah, you think everything's fine because you saw those marvelous dispatches. But the reality counts more than the appearance, believe me. We have to fight off these military plots that the British whip up, and not just in Hong Kong but even more in Canton. They have high hopes for them. The only really good news I heard today is that the British police chief was wounded. Hong has more talent than I thought. Hong's head of the terrorists. The dispatches bring us news of him from time to time: 'Two terrorist attacks yesterday in Hong Kong,' or three attacks or five attacks and so on. Garine backed him all the way. Hong worked with us, he was Garine's assistant. A bright idea that was, spotting that urchin and taking him on! Hong has all the passion of the young for him. He'll get over it. But he's a card, no question. The first time I saw him was in Hong Kong last year. I find out that he's decided to kill the governor with a Browning automatic, this kid who couldn't hit a bull in the ass with a banjo at three feet. He comes to my hotel room, swinging his fat hands like watering cans. A kid, just a kid! 'You know a-bout my pla-ans?' A thick accent, as if he were cutting his syllables in half with his jawbones. I explain that his 'pla-an' is not very smart; for fifteen minutes he listens to me, very annoyed. Then: 'Yes. On-ly it makes no dif-fer-ence, too bad, be-cause I have swo-orn.' So he might as well smash everything. He'd sworn, on a drop of blood from his own finger, in God knows what elegant pagoda. He was very annoyed, very. Even so I was sympathetic: that kind of Chinese is rare. Finally when it's time to go he wiggles his shoulders like a man with fleas and shakes my hand, saying—very slowly—

'When I have been sentenced to capital punishment, you must tell the young to follow my example.' It'd been years since I'd heard 'capital punishment' for 'death.' He was a reader. But without the least sentimentality, as if he'd been saying, 'When I'm dead you must have me cremated.' "

"And the governor?"

"He was going to shoot him down during some ceremony a couple of days later. I can still see myself sitting on my bed stark naked, my hair all shaggy, hot as hell even though it was only ten o'clock, listening to a roar of horns, whistles, and shouts and wondering if it all meant the ceremony's end or the governor's. But Hong was a suspicious character and he'd been deported that same morning. Through all that uproar, the cars and the mobs in the street, I could see his jaw chopping words into syllables and I could hear his voice telling me, 'When I have been sen-tenced to ca-pi-tal pu-nish-ment . . .' I can still hear him. It wasn't empty bragging, you know. For all his fancy talk he really believed he'd be sentenced to death. It'll happen yet. Just a kid."

"Where's he from?"

"The lower depths. I doubt if he ever knew his parents. He replaced them—for the better—with a fellow who sells curios here in Saigon these days, souvenirs, stuff like that. Hey! Would you like to drink a Pernod? A real Pernod?"

"With pleasure."

"Never turn one down. We'll drop in on him day after tomorrow. You'll have a chance to meet one of the men who trained the terrorists. Not many of those left. Are you sleepy?"

"Not particularly."

He calls to the chauffeur; the car whispers toward us. "To Thi-sao's place."

We drive off. A suburb, few streetlamps, patches of

bare black wall, dark canyons where huge dim stars quiver, and formless night given shape here and there by squarish blotches: Annamite booths, where motionless shopkeepers keep watch among stacks of blue bowls. Is Gérard really a former teacher? His personality and speech alter as he tires. I'd really like to know.

We roll along quite fast, and now I'm almost chilly. Wedged into my corner, arms crossed against the breeze, I can still hear the prattle of democracy at dinner, the trite formulas, ridiculous in Europe, harbored here like rusty old steamers; again I see the solemn enthusiasm they ignite among all those men, all those old men. And the Cantonese committee running the whole show takes shape slowly behind the dispatches that Hong Kong cannot censor or suppress, that spring into view one by one like wounds.

1 JULY

HONG KONG: ALL CHINESE HOSPITAL ORDERLIES ARE ON STRIKE.

SHIPS OF THE INDOCHINESE LINE ARE RESTRICTED TO PORT.

TERRORISTS STRUCK AGAIN YESTERDAY.

NO NEWS FROM THE SHAMEEN CONCESSION.

Gloom, boredom, nerves jangling, trying to kill time in this town until the ship sails, when I'd far rather be in Canton. Gérard meets me at the hotel. We have an early luncheon, almost alone in the dining room. He tells me a rounder and more unvarnished tale than before about this Hong, who is now arranging the execution of the British department heads one after another, and about the man we're going to see this afternoon, the man, Gérard says, whom fate made "Hong's midwife." His name is Rebecci. He's a Genoese who's strolled through the Chinese revolution with all the nonchalance of a sleepwalker. When he came to China, years ago, he opened a shop in Shameen;

but he disliked the rich Europeans so much that he gave it up and moved to Canton proper, where Gérard and Garine met him in 1920. To the Chinese he sold gimcracks from cut-rate European emporiums, and he mainly carried little automatons: singing birds, ballerinas, Puss in Boots, that a small coin set in motion; he lived off them. He spoke Cantonese fluently and married a rather pretty local girl, now fat. Around 1895 he'd been a militant anarchist; he disliked talking about that part of his life, which he remembered proudly but sadly and regretted all the more, realizing how ineffectual he'd become since. "Who cares, all that, bygones . . ."

Sometimes Gérard and Garine went to see him about seven in the evening; his large electric sign began to glow; street kids with hair in tufts stared at it, sitting on the ground in a circle. Splashes of daylight lingered on the silks and spangles of his dolls; from the kitchen, the clatter of pans. Stretched out on a wicker chaise longue in the center of his narrow shop. Rebecci dreamed of tours through the interior of the province, with many new automatons. The Chinese would line up at his tent flap; he'd come back rich; he could buy a vast penny arcade where the public might enjoy punching bags, pickaninny dolls with red velvet bellies, electric rifles, scales (your weight and fortune), all kinds of coin-operated machinery, maybe even a bowling alley. . . . When Garine showed up, he emerged from his fantasy as if from a bath, shaking himself; he shook hands and talked about magic. That was his obsession. Not that he was superstitious, strictly speaking; but he was curious. Nothing proved the existence of devils on earth, and particularly in Canton, but nothing proved their absence either, so it was just as well to call them forth. And he called forth many, always with the proper ritual, from those whose names he found in an incomplete Albertus Magnus to those personally known to beggars and servants. He was vouchsafed few demons, but many hints and intimations, which he profited by to astonish his customers or cure them, when opportunity offered, of transient indispositions. He seldom smoked opium, and often at siesta time they saw his white figure strolling, flat hat, thin erect body, floppy trousers like a Zouave's above the cyclist's clips, Charlie Chaplin feet below. He liked to saunter along with a bicycle, and dragged it more than he rode it, an old bicycle but carefully oiled.

He lived surrounded by little girls he'd collected, servants whose principal work was to listen to his stories; his Chinese wife kept a worried eye on them, knowing that he wouldn't turn down a little hanky-panky. Ridden by tropical lusts, he set down *Solomon's Collarbones* only to open *The Rule of the Whip, Slave*, or some other French novel of the same kind. Then he drifted into long reveries, snapping out of them sheepish but yearning, with a shy child's smile: "Monsieur Garine, do you believe the ways of love are dirty?"

"Not at all, old boy. Why?"

"Because, because. It interests me." His library was rounded out by a copy of *Les Misérables* and a few of Jean Grave's pamphlets that he was saving but no longer cared for.

In 1918 he developed an attachment to Hong, who stood out among the Chinese kids who came to listen to him. Soon he gave up ghost stories and taught the boy French (he had no Italian textbook and knew very little English). When Hong could speak it, he learned to read it; then he learned English almost by himself, from scratch, and read everything he could lay his hands on—which wasn't much. Rebecci's experience taught him what books could not. A deep friendship bound them, though it never showed and nobody would have guessed it from Hong's curt comments and Rebecci's shy clumsy irony. A child of grinding poverty, Hong immediately recognized the rare quality of this older friend, who never gave beggars money but always invited them to "have a little drink" (at least until one day when he blew up at a crowd of starving men who shoved into his tiny shop when he was flat broke; blew up and kicked them out), and who, when his brother was clapped into an Italian brig, dropped everything to go live near the prison so he could find ways to deal with the screws and make life easier for him, and now and then kiss him on the mouth to slip him a gold louis. And Rebecci was touched by this Chinese teenager who guffawed at his stories—but in whom he sensed a rare courage, an inflexible love of life, and more than all the rest an intriguing fanaticism. "If they don't kill you too young, you'll do great things."

Hong read Jean Grave, then wanted to know what Rebecci thought of him. Rebecci considered before speaking—that happened rarely—and said, "Got to let me think it over. You know, my boy, Jean Grave isn't just another fellow to me, he's my whole youth. One dreamed dreams, and now one winds up mechanical birds. It was a better time than now, and even so we were wrong. Surprised to hear me say that, hey? No. We were wrong. Because— now you listen to me: when you only have one life to live, you don't try to change the whole world. What's hardest is to know what *you* want. You see, if you toss a bomb at a judge, he dies and something's been done. But if you establish a newspaper to spread your doctrine, nobody gives a damn."

He was a failure. He was not sure how it had happened, but he was a failure. He couldn't go back to Europe: he was too old for manual labor and indifferent to any other kind. And in Canton he was bored, though on the whole . . . Was he bored or was he punishing himself for accepting a life unworthy of his youthful hopes? But wasn't that a fool's reproach? He'd been asked to head up a division of Sun Yat-sen's police; his anarchist principles were still too strong, and he knew that he could never order another man spied on or framed. Later Garine had offered him a job. "No, no, Monsieur Garine. It's very nice of you, but I think it's too late now." Maybe he'd been wrong? But if he wasn't happy, he was, on the whole, at ease among his demons, his books on magnetism, his Chinese wife, Hong, and his mechanical marvels.

Hong thought long about Rebecci's confused self-judgment. The only thing Western thought had stamped indelibly on Hong was the unique character of human life. One life, and one only . . . He'd never felt the fear of death (he never did manage to understand fully what death was: even today dying was not dying, to Hong, but suffering to the limit from a very serious wound), but only the deep, constant fear of spoiling this one life—a life of which no moment once lived could ever be altered.

Still in that bemused state, he became one of Garine's lieutenants. Garine picked him because of the influence his courage had already given him over a fairly large group of young Chinese who made up the party's left wing. Hong was fascinated by Garine but every evening repeated to Rebecci, with a certain mistrust, Garine's opinions and instructions. The old Genoese, lying back on his chaise longue, absorbed in the operation of a paper windmill or the contemplation of one of those water-filled Chinese globes where fantastic gardens flourish, set down his plaything, crossed his hands on his skinny belly, arched his brows in perplexity, and finally answered, "Well, maybe he's right, this Garine. Maybe he's right."

In the end, with civil disorder more and more frequent and Rebecci poorer every day, he took a job in intelligence, with the clearly understood stipulation that he would "not have to rat on anybody." And Garine had sent him to Saigon, where he would be useful.

We've finished lunch and are already in the street, hunched against the heat, Gérard silent. It's time to see Rebecci.

We step into a small bazaar: postcards, Buddhas, cigarettes, Annamite copper work, sketches of Cambodia, fancy aprons, silk cushions with embroidered dragons; hung on the wall up near the ceiling, out of the sunlight, mysterious iron objects. Behind the cash box a fat Chinese woman sits dozing.

"The boss in?"

"No, sir."

"Where?"

"Don' know."

"Bistro?"

"May be Bistro Nam-long."

We cross the street: "Bistro Nam-long" is just opposite. A quiet café; on the ceiling small dun lizards take their siesta. Two servants, bearing opium pipes and the porcelain blocks smokers lay their heads on, pass on the stairway; just in front of us waiters lie sleeping, naked to the waist, hair flopping on a folded arm. Lying alone on a black wooden bench, a man stares into the middle distance, nodding gently. When he see Gérard, he stands up. I'm startled: I've been expecting a Garibaldian sort of fellow and this is a little dried-up man with gnarled fingers and straight graying hair in a soup-bowl cut.

"Here's a man who hasn't had a Pernod for years," Gérard says, gesturing at me.

"Good," Rebecci says. "Let's do it."

He leaves. We follow him. "Garine nicknamed him Punch," Gérard murmurs as we cross the street.

We go into his shop and up to the second floor. The

[23]

Chinese woman snaps awake, watches us pass, and goes back to sleep. The room is huge. In the middle, a bed within mosquito netting; along the walls, numerous objects covered with flowered cloth. Rebecci leaves us. We hear the screech of a key in a lock, a chest shut sharply, water flowing from a faucet and gurgling in a glass. "I'm going downstairs for a minute," Gérard says. "I have to chat with his wife, if she's not too fast asleep. She enjoys it."

It's a long minute. Rebecci comes back first, still silent, carrying a bottle, sugar, water, and three glasses on a tray. Without a word he sits down and mixes the three Pernods. After a moment: "Well, now! I've retired, you understand."

"Rebecci," Gérard cries, coming up the stairs at last, smoothing his beard, "our comrade expects anecdotes about your son in spirit! I hung around for a while down there—had the feeling we were being followed. No."

He hasn't noticed how Rebecci's face changed when he mentioned Hong. "If I didn't know you like I do, you'd have the back of my hand for that! Don't joke about him!"

"What's the matter with you?"

"You picked the wrong day."

"What day?"

Rebecci shrugs angrily. "Were you at the president's banquet this noon?"

"No."

"Why the hell not?"

"We had an appointment for five o'clock."

"Oh. Then that's it. Well, you better ask him about Hong. He'll tell you Hong's been nabbed."

"The British? The Whites? When?"

"Last night, he said. Maybe two hours after the last cables." He taps his glass several times with his spoon, then quaffs his Pernod. "Some other day, I might not mind. And the Pernod is always here for friends."

2 JULY

STEAMING DOWNRIVER

You'd have thought their anxiety would deepen as we approached our destination. Not at all: the dominant mood aboard is torpor. Every hour—as we make our way along the low banks of the river through dense, steamy air, our hands dripping sweat—Hong Kong becomes more real, more than just a name or a place somewhere along the shore or a rocky landscape. We all feel its life stirring. No true anxiety now, but a confused mood, the soporific regularity of the ship's motion contrasting with each man's knowledge that these are his last moments of liberty. Our bodies are still our own; our uneasiness is abstract. A strange interlude, during which ancient animal presences take possession of the whole ship. An almost cheerful daze, a nerveless calm. Not yet seeing, knowing only news reports, not yet *possessed*.

5 JULY
5 P.M.

A GENERAL STRIKE HAS BEEN CALLED IN HONG KONG.

5:30

THE GOVERNMENT DECLARES MARTIAL LAW.

9 P.M.

IN THE ROADS, HONG KONG

We've just passed the lighthouse. No one's even trying to sleep; men and women both crowd the decks. Lemonade, whiskey-and-soda. Reflected in the water, a dazzle of light bulbs outlines Chinese restaurants. Above us, the overwhelming mass of the famous rock, black below,

[25]

sloping as it rises, finally rounding off in an Asiatic double hump against the stars, fringed by a light mist. It's not a silhouette snipped out of paper, but a solid and profound thing, like primal matter, like black earth. A line of lights (a road?) circles the higher of the two humps, the Peak, like a necklace. All we can see of the houses is an unbelievably dense seeding of thronged lights, almost merging above the trembling outlines of the Chinese restaurants, thinning out and dimming as they rise like the black rock itself, finally lost among the full, glittering stars. In the bay many large ships lie sleeping, their brilliant tiers of portholes reflecting zigzag, overlapping the city's glow on the warm waters. All these lights in the sea and the Chinese sky turn my imagination not to the white man's creative energies but rather to a Polynesian celebration, one of those feasts when painted gods are honored by a great discharge of fireflies, flung to the island night like seeds. . . .

Wiping out the scene, a strange, tall screen passes before us, the only sound a single-stringed guitar: a junk's sail. The air is tepid—and so calm!

Suddenly the landscape of glittering dots ceases its advance. All engines stop. The anchors drop with a deafening clank and clatter of running iron. Tomorrow morning at seven the police will board. Nobody allowed ashore.

MORNING

Deckhands carry our baggage to the company launch. Not one coolie comes to dicker for the job. We glide across the surface of the sea, hardly even rolling on the dense, lagoonlike water. We round a small cape bristling with chimneys and semaphores, and abruptly we see the business section: tall buildings lining the docks, a Hamburg or London skyline crushed flat by a vast cone of thick greenery, and a sky rippling as if the limpid air were rising from an oven. The launch makes fast to the loading dock at the railway station, where only days ago trains left for Canton.

Still no coolies. They say the Company's asked the big European hotels to send porters. . . . Nobody. With the help of the sailors, the passengers hoist their baggage, straining and sweating.

Here's the main avenue. Boundary between the rock and the sea, the city built on the one and hanging over the other is a crescent; this avenue, cut at right angles by all the sloping roads that connect the docks with the Peak, runs like the spine of a great palm leaf. Usually all the island's activities are concentrated here. Today the avenue is deserted and silent. At long intervals pairs of British volunteers,* sticking together and wary, dressed like boy scouts, make their way to the market to distribute meat or vegetables. Wooden clogs clack in the distance. No white women. No cars.

And here are the Chinese shops, jewelry stores, jade merchants, luxury items; I see fewer British firms; and as the road curves suddenly, I see none. It's a hairpin turn; the road seems to close itself off like a courtyard. Everywhere, on every floor of every front, characters: black, red, gilt, painted on vertical panels or fastened over doorways, enormous or tiny, at eye level or high against the rectangle of sky, they surround me like a swarm of insects. Deep within great dark three-walled caverns, shopkeepers in long robes, sitting on their counters, gaze out at the street. As soon as I come into sight, they turn their small eyes toward knickknacks that have hung from the ceilings for millennia, dried cuttlefish, squid, ordinary fish, black sausages, ducks lacquered the color of ham; or to the sacks of seed and cases of loam-flecked eggs on the

* Not *ad hoc*. British volunteer forces go back to 1854. (Tr.)

floor. Dense, narrow rays of sunlight strike them, full of tawny dust. If I look back, I find them brooding at me, heavily, hatefully.

In front of the Chinese banks flaunting gilt signs—banks closed off, like prisons or butcher shops, behind iron gratings—British soldiers stand guard; more than once I hear the smack of a rifle butt on the sidewalk. An empty symbol. The dogged English, irresistible in their house-to-house conquest of this Chinese city built on Chinese rock, are helpless against the passive hostility of three hundred thousand Chinese who have decided to stop being the conquered. Useless rifles. The British are being denied not merely profit, but battle.

Four o'clock. A restless siesta thanks to a fan that hardly turns, because of a cutback at the power plant. It's still extremely hot, and in the streets—made of a shiny asphalt that reflects the blue sky—a heat hotter than the air rises with the dust. The Kuomintang's deputy agent here is supposed to bring me documents. The principal agent, a Balt, has just been deported. I may see Klein, the German who organized the strike.

All I know about this deputy is that he's called Meunier, was once a mechanic in Paris, and was a machine-gun sergeant during the war. The look of him, at the door of his simple colonial house at the foot of the Peak, surprises me: I thought he'd be an older man and he doesn't seem more than thirty-five. He's a tall, clean-shaven man, sturdy, and he has the look of a mischievous rabbit, with a very short upper lip beneath a delicate nose, tiny lively eyes, and wild curly hair. He's cordial, talkative, obviously happy to be speaking French, sunk in his wicker arm-chair with two tall sweaty mint drinks in front of him.

After a few moments he lets himself go: "Ah, it's a lovely sight, the old English bulldog, the genuine article,

Hong Kong itself, rotting on its feet, food for worms! You saw the streets, right, if you just came in this morning? Not too bad. In fact very damn good. But that's nothing, buddy, nothing, take it from me! You have to see it from inside to appreciate the real beauty of it."

"And what do you see from inside?"

"Well, a lot of things. Prices, for instance. Houses worth five thousand dollars a year ago are on the market for fifteen hundred. And the police making bullshit announcements. Like when they spread the word they'd collared Hong. Hah!"

"It wasn't true?"

"True! A flat lie."

"But in Saigon everybody thought . . ."

"They never run out of tall stories. Hong's in Canton, perfectly safe."

"Do you know Borodin?"

"I figure Clemenceau looked like that when he was forty or forty-five. Full of experience. The only thing I hold against him is, he's a little too fond of the Russians."

"Garine?"

"He did a great thing just lately: he made active propaganda agents out of the strikers in Canton—they were living off money that he and Borodin finally made the government cough up. An army of them! But he's beginning to look like a corpse, Garine is. Malaria, dysentery, God knows what.

"Another drink? An armchair's the best place to be, this time of day. Hey, while I think of it—here's the documents. Take them now, that way you won't forget them. That was a good idea the English had, to man the Canton–Hong Kong shuttle with sailors off a battlewagon! Klein'll be along in a while: you're going upriver together. He wasn't going to leave for a few days more but he's been spotted, and if I can believe my tips from the police he'd be better off to lam out of here fast. I probably haven't got too long myself."

"You're sure I won't be searched when I leave tonight?"

"No reason for it. You're in transit, and they know your papers are in order. They also know that searches are the same thing as useless. Of course, you'll take the usual precautions. They'd have to fling you into the slammer to get anything out of you, and there's no danger of that yet. Deportation at the worst."

"That's crazy."

"No, it's simple. They prefer to work through their Intelligence Service, and in a pinch discreet diplomatic intervention. They're in a very peculiar position. Legally they're not at war with Canton. They may try to dig something up, but they're not that interested in hanging on to you and Klein; to them you're small fry. Do you know him? Klein? Well, no, you couldn't, you just got here."

His tone makes me ask, "What have you got against him?"

"He's a little funny. But he's a real professional, really good. I've seen him operate, and he sure knows how to set off a string of strikes! And speaking of work, I meant to tell you just now that one of the times Garine showed class was when he organized the military academy. Whampoa. That was no joke. That, I admire. Make a soldier out of a Chinaman, that was never easy. Out of a rich Chinaman, even harder. He recruited a thousand men, and made them the backbone of a small army. In a year there'll be ten times as many, and then I don't see what Chinese army could stand up to them. Maybe Chang Tso-lin's, but I'm not so sure. And if the British want to send out an expeditionary force (assuming that the comrades back there'll let them sail), then we'll have some fun.

"To round up those cadets was nothing; but he gave them ranks and insignia, he made them respected. Well, even that can be done. But he introduced them to a vice not very popular in China, called courage. I take off my hat to him; I could never have done it. I know he had a lot of help from Galen and the commandant at the academy, Chiang Kai-shek. It was Chiang, with Garine, who rounded up the first serious cadets. My God, he did it the way the British built this city: man by man, courage by courage, pleading, demanding, agitating. And it couldn't have been fun. Going around to see old gargoyles with a little-fingernail that long, and taking their spoiled brats away from them. I don't know how they did it. I know it helped him when the son of the former Manchu viceroy was sent to Whampoa. And his own family helped, I heard. Anyway they did a good job. And to pound it into people's heads that the cadets aren't soldiers, but servants of the revolution, that was good work too. And we saw the results at Shameen on the twenty-fifth."

"Not so brilliant."

"Because they didn't take Shameen? Do you think they really wanted to take it?"

"You have any serious information about that?"

"You'll hear more about it there. I think it was mainly aimed at Ch'eng-tai. The more time goes by, the more we need to shock him with a fait accompli. Remains to be seen. What we've already seen is, when the machine guns opened up on our men, the mob scattered like rabbits, as usual, but fifty-odd men charged the guns: all cadets. They found them thirty yards from the guns—all dead, of course. I have a crazy notion that something in China changed that day."

"Why do you say the attack on Shameen was aimed at Ch'eng-tai?"

[31]

"I said *maybe*. I get the feeling that we and he aren't working together too well anymore, and I'm especially leery of his friend the governor. Wu Han-min."

"Gérard was worried too. Is Ch'eng-tai as popular as ever?"

"No. A lot less, lately."

"But what does he *do*?"

"He doesn't hold office. But he's the head of a lot of secret societies that make up the best part of the Kuomintang's right wing. Listen, old buddy, Gandhi never held office either, and when he ordered the Hartal, told the Hindus to go out on strike, they went out even with the Prince of Wales arriving, and the Prince went through Calcutta like it was a school for deaf-mutes. Afterward a lot of Hindus lost their jobs, and more or less died of hunger, naturally, but just the same. . . . Out here moral force is as real and as sure as that table or this chair."

"But Gandhi's a saint."

"Maybe. Nobody knows. Gandhi's a myth, and that's what's important. Ch'eng-tai too. You don't find men like that in Europe."

"And the government?"

"Of Canton?"

"Yes."

"Like the beam on a scale, oscillating, trying not to swing from Garine and Borodin—they have the police and the unions—to Ch'eng-tai—he has nothing but he's just as solid. Anarchy, old buddy, is when the government's weak, not when there's no government at all. In the first place, there's always government; when things go badly there's more than one, that's all. This government now, Garine would like to see them up to their neck in the fight: he wants them to issue his damn decree! That would panic the British! Hong Kong without one ship laying over, Hong Kong banned to ships touching in China, is a dead port, a ghost town. Think about it: just at the *possibility*, they asked for military intervention. Ha! If he gets them to do it, he'll be a genius. But it's stalled. It's stalled."

"Why?"

"Well . . . hard to say. You understand, the government wants to be partners with us, even run things if they can; if they follow us too far behind, they're afraid they'll be eaten alive, either by the British or by us. It would be one thing if we were only fighting Hong Kong; but the interior! The interior! That's where they want us. Have to take a good hard look. . . ."

We sip our mint in a silence rare in the tropics, and unmarred even by the fan, which is off. A silence unbroken by the singsong cries of wandering merchants, unbroken by firecrackers, birds, cicadas. A gentle breeze off the bay sways the mats hung across the windows, and reveals a triangle of white wall covered with sleeping lizards, and brings us the smell of the road, tar cooking; now the lonely call of a distant horn, solitary and muffled, rises from the sea. . . .

Visibly weary, Klein shows up at about five and promptly collapses into a groaning wicker armchair, his hands heavy on his knees. He's a big man, broad-shouldered, and his striking features surprise me: now and then you come across the type in England, but hardly ever in Germany. Pale eyes beneath shaggy brows, flat nose, the formidable line of a downturned mouth accented by deep wrinkles from nose to chin—in that broad, flat face is something of the boxer, the bulldog, and the butcher. Back in Europe he was doubtless ruddy—his cheeks bear the tiny marks of acne rosacea—but here's he's tanned like all the Europeans. At first he speaks French, with a thick north-German accent that lends a singsong, almost Belgian, note to his slightly husky voice; exhausted, he stumbles, barely making sense, and soon decides to speak German. Every little while Meunier recapitulates their conversation in French:

The general strike in Canton is two weeks old. It is intended to consolidate the power of the left-wing leadership, weaken the moderates, and at the same time attack the rich anti-Kuomintang merchants who trade with the British and are the principal source of Hong Kong's wealth. Borodin and Garine have to keep 50,000 men alive out of the strike fund, taxes raised in Canton, and remittances from the innumerable revolutionary Chinese in "the colonies." The general strike order in Hong Kong, laying off 100,000 workers, forced the Cantonese government to allot strike pay to so many that the appropriations will be exhausted in a few days. The allotments have already run out for unskilled laborers. But in this city, even if the British secret police have been powerless to stamp out Cantonese organizations, the uniformed police, reinforced by volunteer machine-gun squads, are too strong for a riot to succeed. Violence these last few days has been limited to street fights. So the workers will have to go back to work to survive—which the British are waiting for.

Garine is currently in charge of propaganda and knows just as well as Borodin what a critical point this is, how close this colossal strike is—even though its impact has stunned every European in the Far East—to collapse. Both men are restricted to advisory roles, and they're up against the ruling Committee's formal refusal to issue decrees they'd counted on. Klein says Ch'eng-tai is using all his influence to tie their hands. Also, the anarchists are picking up strength dangerously—which was easy enough to foresee—and a series of terrorist attacks has begun in Canton. And finally, the Kuomintang's ancient enemy

General Ch'en Chiung-ming is in the process (thanks to British subsidies) of raising a new army to march on the city.

Our ship is under way.

All I can see of the island now is a silhouette pricked out by innumerable tiny lights and slowly shrinking, dark beneath a bland sky. Immense billboards loom above the houses—advertisements for the large British corporations, billboards that only a month ago ruled over the city's night sky. Electricity is precious now and no longer quickens them; their colors fade into the evening. A sudden bend in the river replaces them with a bare stretch of the mountainous Chinese coast, clay soil under rashes of short grass, the landscape disappearing into a night swarming with mosquitoes, like a night three thousand years ago. And darkness blots out that island eaten away by intelligent termites who leave it with its imperial façade, but too weak to brandish more than great black billboards, burnt-out symbols of its wealth.

Silence. Absolute silence, and stars. Soundless, faceless, junks pass below us, borne on the current we breast. Nothing earthly now about the mountains that surround us, or the water that neither chuckles nor slaps, or this dead river that plunges into the night like a blind man; nothing human about the boats we pass, unless maybe lanterns shining so feebly astern that they scarcely reflect on the water.

"It's not the same smell." Full night has fallen. Klein is beside me. He speaks French, almost whispering: "Not the same. Have you ever sailed the rivers at night? In Europe, I mean."

"Yes."

"How different, isn't it, how different. Back home the

[35]

silence of the night means peace. Here you expect machine-gun fire. Am I right?"

He's right. This is a night of truce: we sense armed men lurking in the silence. Klein shows me trembling points of light barely visible: "Those are ours." Still he talks quietly, confidentially. "Can't see a thing along here. Blacked out. Look. On the benches. On display."

Behind us on deck are a dozen Europeans from firms with branches in Shameen. They're on their way to join the merchant volunteers. Now they're sitting in a semi-circle around two young women sent along by a newspaper, they say (or by the police?). The young men are storming the foe with sneers. "So they asked the Kremlin for a crystal coffin like Lenin's, but the Russians sent glass." (They must be talking about Sun Yat-sen.) "And another time . . ."

Klein shrugs. "Those are only fools." He lays a hand on my arm and looks me in the eye. "You know, during the Paris Commune they arrested a fat man. So he shouts, 'But gentlemen, I was never political!' A smart guy answers, 'Exactly!' and bashes him."

"Meaning?"

"That it doesn't always have to be the same people who suffer. I remember a celebration one time, where I was watching some . . . some creatures like these. Ach! for a few cartridges to wipe out that . . . I don't know just how to say it. That smile! The look on all the smug faces of people who never had to miss a meal! Yah, just to let them know that something called human life really exists! It's a rare thing, *ein Mensch*, a real man!"

I hold back an answer. Is he talking out of sympathy or need? His low voice is almost toneless, and under the thin whine of mosquitoes he sounds almost hoarse. His hands are trembling; he hasn't slept for three days. He's half drunk with fatigue.

Aft, behind a barred gate guarded by two Hindu soldiers, the Chinese passengers gamble and smoke quietly. Turning, Klein stares at the thick bars. "Do you know how I got through the worst ordeals in prison? the most inhuman? I dreamed about poisoning the whole city. I could have done it, too. Could have done the reservoirs after they let me out, and I knew where I could lay my hands on a whole lot of cyanide, through a buddy, an electrician. When it hurt too much, I dreamed about the ways and means. I imagined every detail. That made it all easier. Convicts, epileptics, syphilitics, cripples—they're not like other people. The ones who *cannot* accept."

A pulley falls to the deck; it clangs; he jumps. He catches his breath and goes on bitterly: "I'm too nervous tonight. Dog-tired. Those memories stay with you. At the center of all the misery there's often a man. You have to hang on to that man after the misery's licked. That's not easy.

"What's the revolution to them, to the world in general? The *Stimmung* of the revolution—damned important!— what is it, anyway? I'll tell you: nobody knows. But mainly it's because there's too much poverty, not just the lack of money but—it's always because there's these rich people who live life and all the rest who don't live it." His voice is harsher. He's leaning forward, both elbows planted on the rail, and as he ends his sentence he shrugs his broad shoulders forward, as another might pound a fist. "It's changed out here! When the merchant volunteers tried to bring back the old ways, the neighborhood burned for three days. Women with bound feet scurried like penguins." He pauses, his eyes blank, then says, "And it's all so goddam stupid. The dead. In Munich, in Odessa. A lot more. All so goddam stupid."

He says "schtupid" with disgust.

"They lie there like rabbits, or something out of a picture book. It isn't tragic. No. It's schtupid. Most of all when they have mustaches. You have to keep telling yourself that these are real men that've been killed. It's hard to believe."

He falls silent again, his body hunched heavily over the rail. Around the shaded deck lamp mosquitoes and insects swirl thicker than ever. Unseeing, we sense the banks of the invisible river of shadow, lightless save for the clinging reflection of our own bulbs. Tall shapes bulk vaguely here and there in the night sky: fishermen's nets on poles, maybe. "Klein."

"*Was?* What?"

"Why don't you go to bed?"

"Too tired. Too hot below."

I fetch a deck chair and set it up beside him. He stretches out slowly, without a word, lays his head on his arm, and lies still, in the grip of sleep or brutish exhaustion. Except for the officer of the watch, the Hindu sentries, and myself, everyone's asleep: the Chinese on their baggage behind the barred gate, whites on deck chairs or in their cabins. When the engine's rumble diminishes, all we can hear is snoring sleepers and one old Chinese who coughs, coughs, racked by endless fits of coughing because all over the ship the boys have lit sticks of incense to drive off the mosquitoes.

I retreat to my cabin. But the throes of sleeplessness plague me there too: migraine, weariness, chills. I wash my face in great gouts of water (not easy: the faucets are tiny), switch on the fan, open the porthole.

Sitting on my berth with nothing much to do, one by one I pull an assortment of papers from my pockets. Ads for tropical drugstores, old letters, stationery embellished with the little tricolor of the Messageries Maritimes. I shred them all with a drunkard's finicky care and toss them overboard through the porthole. In another pocket, old letters from the man they call Garine. I decided not to leave them in my suitcase. Simple prudence. And this? This is a list of the documents Meunier gave me. But here are two that Meunier's set apart even on his list. The first is a copy of a memo from the Intelligence Service about Ch'eng-tai, with notes by our agents. The second ˇis a copy of a Hong Kong police report on Garine.

I lock and bolt the cabin door. Then I dig into my shirt pocket for the fat envelope Meunier gave me. The report I'm looking for is the last one. It's long and in code. At the top of page one, URGENT. Anyway the code is attached.

Moved by curiosity and even a twinge of uneasiness, I start decoding. What is he now, this man who's been my friend for years? It's been over five years since I saw him. During this trip not a day has passed without some memory of him—either because somebody mentioned him to me or because I could sense his tactics behind every bulletin. I picture him as I saw him last in Marseilles, but the face is a composite of his successive faces: large gray eyes, hard and almost lashless, a narrow, slightly hooked nose (his mother was Jewish), and gouged into his cheeks two fine, sharp wrinkles that tug down the corners of his mouth, as on so many Roman busts. It's not those sharp furrows that give his face its character, but rather the mouth, the unyielding, tight lips working with the motion of the strong jaw. An energetic, nervous mouth.

I'm tired: memories fall into place around each sentence I laboriously decode. I hear voices. Something of the drunkard's obsessiveness in me tonight.

Pierre Garin alias Garine or Harine. Born in Geneva 5 November 1892 to Maurice Garin, Swiss citizen, and his wife Sophia Alexandrovna Mirsky, Russian.

He was born in 1894. Is he pretending to be older?

[3 9]

Militant anarchist. Convicted of conspiracy in an anarchist case in Paris, 1914.

No. He was never a "militant anarchist." In 1914—at twenty—he was still under the spell of his literary studies, mainly their revelation of tremendous conflicting forces in life. ("What books are worth writing, aside from memoirs?") He was indifferent to systems, and had decided to go along with whichever one circumstances imposed on him. What he was hoping to find among the anarchists (though half of them were police spies) and the extreme socialists was some hope of a general upheaval. Often I heard him, just back from some meeting (where, naïvely, he showed up wearing a Barclay cap), talk with scornful irony of the men he'd just seen who claimed to be working for the greater happiness of mankind. "Those fatheads just want to show how right they are. But practically speaking there's only one 'right' that isn't a joke: the most efficient use of force." That idea was popular then, and wove itself easily into the woof of his imagination, already warped by Saint-Just.*

In general, people considered him ambitious. But an ambition isn't real unless it spurs its victim to action; and he lacked the will to do, to plan a series of overt acts, to identify his very life with them. The necessary strategies were still beyond his character and intelligence. But deep down he felt a stubborn, persistent craving for power. "It's not so much a man's soul that makes him a leader as it is success," he told me one day. And added ironically, "Worse luck!" And a few days later (he was reading the *Memorial*): "And nothing feeds charisma like success. On St. Helena Napoleon was so far gone that he said, 'Still, what a novel my life would make!' Genius rots too."

* Ambitious, ruthless, articulate supporter of Robespierre in the French Revolution. (Tr.)

He knew that the ambition driving him was different from so many that spark briefly in adolescent hearts because he was giving over his life to it; because he was accepting every risk implied. He craved power for its own sake, not for the wealth, notoriety, or respect it might bring him. And when his young man's fancy focused on power, it was in an almost physical manner. No fantasies: a kind of tightness, tension, expectation. The ridiculous image of a coiled animal, ready to spring, haunted him. So finally he came to see the exercise of power as a sort of relief, a deliverance.

He was prepared to lay his life on the line. Courageous, he knew that death cuts all losses; young, he was indifferent to death; and he had no clear idea yet of what he might win. Slowly a definite resolve replaced the confused hopes of adolescence, though it couldn't fully dominate a character whose distinguishing obsession was still violence—if only the lighthearted notion of violence possible at twenty, when experience is still limited to the philosophical.

But soon enough he found himself in brutal contact with real life. One morning in Lausanne I got a letter from one of our friends telling me that Pierre had been implicated in an alleged abortion; and two days later a note from Pierre himself, somewhat more detailed.

Among the anarchists there was plenty of birth-control agitation, but very few midwives who would perform abortions as a matter of principle; and a natural compromise followed—the midwives would bring on an abortion "for the cause" in return for a fat fee. Several times Pierre, half on principle and half in vanity, had put up the money that poor young women couldn't raise. He enjoyed a handsome legacy from his mother (which the police report omits); all they had to do was ask him; they asked him often. Acting on a tip, the police arrested several midwives, and Pierre was indicted as an accessory.

[41]

At first he was astounded. He knew that what he'd done was against the law, but the monstrosity of a legal judgment passed on actions of that kind left him shaken. Furthermore, he couldn't really imagine what form such a judgment might take. I saw him often then; he was free on bail. The legal confrontation was of no interest to him; he denied nothing. And the trial was like a debate with an automaton of primitive reasoning powers; it was conducted by a bearded, indifferent judge whose primary concern was the reduction of facts to a sort of judicial allegory.

One day when the judge asked him a question, he answered, "What difference does it make?"

"Well," the judge said, "it can be important in passing sentence."

That shook Garine again. The notion of a genuine verdict and sentence had not yet sunk in. So even though he was a man of courage, and scorned those who were to judge him, he got busy and asked all the friends he could reach to use their influence in his favor. Intolerable to stake his life on this tattered, worthless card that he himself hadn't chosen.

Busy in Lausanne, I missed the trial.

All through it he felt like a character in a fantasy, not a dream but a crazy comedy, a bit tawdry and altogether lunatic. Only the theater can be as stylized as a courtroom. The words of the juror's oath, read out by the judge in a tired schoolmaster's voice, had a surprising effect on those twelve placid shopkeepers, suddenly impassioned, aching to mete out justice, to shun error, girding themselves to assiduous judgment. It never bothered them for a moment that they hadn't the slightest understanding of the facts they were about to weigh. The self-assurance of certain witnesses, the hesitations of others, the judge's bearing as he questioned them (an expert at a meeting of laymen),

[4 2]

and his hostility toward certain defense witnesses—all that showed Pierre how little connection there was between the points at issue and this charade. At first he was quite interested; the play of the defense fascinated him. But he tired of it, and while the last witnesses were being heard, he told himself, smiling, "To pass judgment is obviously not to understand, because if you understand, you couldn't judge." The judge's and prosecutor's efforts to identify the events at issue with the notion of crime—that notion at least familiar to the jurors—seemed such a parody at one point that he broke out laughing. But justice was so impressive in that courtroom, the magistrates, police, and crowd were so perfectly of one mind, that indignation seemed misplaced. His smile fading, Pierre suffered the same sense of exasperated impotence, scorn, and disgust as in the face of a fanatical mob, as at all large-scale manifestations of human absurdity.

He **was** irritated by his supernumerary's part. He felt like a walk-on thrust onstage by some obscure motivation in a play of unusually spurious psychology performed for a stupid audience. Discouraged, infuriated, beyond even the desire to tell these fools how wrong they were, he awaited the final curtain, and the end of his ordeal, with mingled impatience and resignation.

Only when he was alone in his cell (where they'd locked him up two days before the trial began) did the meaning of it all begin to seep through to him. There he understood that a verdict was to be rendered; that his freedom was at stake; that this whole shoddy performance might end with him sentenced to a degrading, grublike existence for an indefinite period. Prison was less ominous now that he'd experienced it; nevertheless the prospect of a long stretch, however he might manage to ease his lot, inspired a gloom all the thicker because he was so helpless.

Sentenced to six months' imprisonment.

No need to be melodramatic: a telegram from Pierre told me that sentence had been suspended.

Here's the letter he wrote me:

I don't see society as bad, as susceptible of improvement; I see it as absurd. That's entirely different. I fought hard for an acquittal from those fools, or at least to stay out of jail, because I have a sense of my destiny—not of myself, of my destiny—that cannot accept prison for such a weird reason.

Absurd. And I don't mean unreasonable. I don't care about transforming society. It's not the general absence of justice that bothers me, but something deeper, the impossibility of pledging my allegiance to any social order, whatever it is. I'm asocial as I'm an atheist, and in the same way. None of that would matter a damn if I were an academic, but I know I'll have to spend my life on the fringes of *some* social order, and that I'll never be able to accept it without renouncing all that I truly am.

And a short while later:

There's a passion deeper than all the others, a passion in which the obstacles to be overcome are utterly unimportant. A perfectly hopeless passion—one of the strongest props of power.

Sent to the French Foreign Legion in August 1914, deserts at the end of 1915.

Not true. He wasn't sent to the Legion; he enlisted. Impossible to attend the war as a spectator. Its remote underlying causes were of no interest to him; the German invasion of Belgium merely looked like a sensible way to fight a war. He picked the Legion because it was so easy to join. He sought combat; he found the inertia of millions of men who were passive amid the uproar. The idea of quitting incubated for a while, and hatched as a firm resolve one day when they were issued new weapons for

[44]

mopping up in the trenches. The Legionnaires had now and then been issued dirks, soldiers' weapons anyway; that day they got new knives with brown wooden handles and broad blades, ignoble and disgusting versions of butcher knives.

I don't know how he slipped away and crossed into Switzerland, but this time he worked shrewdly and carefully, and was listed as missing in action. (That's why I'm so surprised to see desertion specified in the British memo. True, he has no reason nowadays to keep it secret.)

Loses his capital in various financial speculations.

He was always a gambler.

Runs a pacifist publishing house in Zurich, thanks to his many languages. Is there associated with Russian revolutionaries.

With a Swiss father and a Russian mother, he speaks German, French, Russian, and English, this last learned in school. What he ran was not a publishing house but the translation service of a firm whose publications were not necessarily pacifist.

As the police report says, from time to time he hung around with young members of the Bolshevik group. He saw quickly that this time he was among technicians and not preachers. The group was barely hospitable; only the memory of his trial, not forgotten in these circles, spared him a nuisance's reception. But not committed to their line (he'd never wanted to join the party, knowing that he couldn't tolerate the discipline and not believing in any imminent revolution), he never established deeper relations than companionship. The young men interested him more than their leaders. All he knew of the leaders was their speeches, orations delivered in conversational tones in small smoky cafés for twenty-odd comrades slumped over the tables, only their faces attentive. He never saw Lenin. If the Bolsheviks' taste for rebellion, and their techniques, tempted him, the doctrinaire vocabulary exasperated him, and most of all the dogmatism that weighed them down. The truth was, he was one of those whose revolutionary fervor is born only of revolution itself—one of those for whom revolution is primarily action.

When the Russian revolution broke out, he was amazed. One by one his comrades left Zurich, promising they'd find a way to get him to Russia. It seemed both necessary and right to go there, and he saw his friends off without envy but with an odd feeling that he was being cheated.

After the October revolution he burned to make the trip; he wrote, but party leaders had more to do than answer letters from Switzerland and enroll amateurs. He suffered in dismal rage. He wrote to me:

God knows I've seen fanatics, men possessed by an idea, attached to their children, their money, their mistresses, even their hopes, as they are to their arms and legs; intoxicated, haunted, forgetting everything in the defense or pursuit of their passion! If I said I wanted a million, people would call me greedy; a hundred million, fanciful but perhaps forceful; and if I say that I see my youth as the card I'm betting on, they seem to take me for a visionary simpleton. And when I make that bet, believe me, I'll make it like the poor man at Monte Carlo who's ready to kill himself if he loses. If I could cheat, I'd cheat. To be in love and not see that you're pouring your heart out to a woman who doesn't give a damn—that's normal, you can kid yourself about that all you want. But you can't kid yourself about the game of life. It seems fairly simple. Seems it's riskier to concentrate on your own destiny than on day-to-day problems or hopes or dreams. Well, I plan to do my homework—if I can only dig up the price of the first step, that I squandered like a damn fool!

Sent to Canton at the end of 1918 by the Communist International.

Stupid. He knew one of my buddies in school, Lambert, much older then we, whose parents—French bureaucrats —had been friends of my own parents, business people in Haiphong. Like almost all the European children in that city, Lambert had been raised by a Cantonese nursemaid and spoke the dialect, as I did. He'd gone out to Tonkin again in early 1914. Quickly discouraged by colonial life, he went on to China, where he became one of Sun Yat-sen's colleagues, and he never came back to join his regiment when war broke out. He was in regular correspondence with Pierre and had long since promised to find a way to bring him out to Canton. Pierre wasn't sure how good the promise was but studied Chinese nonetheless, often discouraged by it. One day in June 1918 he had a letter from Lambert: "If you really want to leave Europe, let me know. I can have you sent for: eight hundred dollars a month." He answered immediately. And at the end of November, after the armistice, he received another letter with a check on a Marseilles bank for slightly more than the price of the ticket.

I had a little ready money then. I went as far as Marseilles with him.

A day spent sauntering through the city. A Mediterranean atmosphere, all work seems voluntary; under a pale winter sun streets gleam, speckled by the blue overcoats of soldiers awaiting discharge. . . . His features have hardly changed: traces of the war in his taut, thinner cheeks creased by tiny vertical wrinkles that accent the flash of the blue eyes, the curve of the narrow mouth, and the depth of the furrows that extend it.

We've been walking and talking for hours. One emotion consumes him: impatience. He hides it, but it shows in every gesture, even in the jerky rhythm of his speech. "Do you really know what remorse can be?" he asks abruptly.

I come to a halt, startled.

"Real remorse. Not something out of a book or a play. A strong dislike of yourself, yourself of another year. A feeling that can only spring from some serious act—and serious acts aren't committed by accident."

"That depends."

"No. When a man's finished with his youth and still suffers remorse, it must be because he doesn't know how to profit by experience." And noticing my surprise: "I tell you this apropos of the Russians."

We've just passed a bookstore window full of Russian novelists.

"There's a flaw in what they wrote, and that flaw is something like remorse. All those writers have one fault: they never killed anybody. If their characters suffer after killing, it's because the world's hardly changed for them. I said *hardly*. In real life I believe they'd see the world completely transformed, its perspectives altered, not the world of a man who has 'committed a crime' but the world of a man who has killed. This untransformed world of theirs—let's say not transformed enough, if you like— I can't believe it's real. For an assassin there's no such thing as crime, there's only murder. If he's sane, of course." And after a pause he goes on: "Even when you can't stand yourself, it's never as bad as you make it out. To bind yourself to any great line of action and not back off, to be haunted by it, besotted with it, may be . . ." But he shrugs and leaves his sentence there.

"Too bad you're not a believer. You'd have made a good mission——"

"No! First because the things I consider contemptible don't humiliate me. They're part of man. I accept them as I accept being cold in winter. I have no desire to bring them under law. And I'd have made a bad missionary for a second reason: I don't love mankind. I don't even love

[48]

the poor, in other words the people I'm going to fight for."

"You like them better than the others, and it comes to the same thing."

"Not on your life!"

"What, not on your life—that you don't prefer them or that it doesn't come to the same thing?"

"I prefer them, but only because they're the down-trodden. On the whole, yes, they have more heart, more humanity than the others—the virtues of the conquered. I'm sure of one thing: all I feel for the bourgeoisie I came out of is hate and disgust. And I'm also sure the others will turn rotten when we've won. We have the battle in common, and that's a lot less complicated."

"Then why are you leaving?"

This time he comes to a halt.

"Have you lost your mind?"

"I doubt it. Somebody would have noticed."

"I'm leaving because I have no desire to go back and make a fool of myself in a courtroom, on a serious charge this time. My life doesn't interest me. That's clear, straight-forward, categorical. What I want—are you listening?— is a certain form of power. Either I'll find it, or too bad for me."

"Too bad because you've failed?"

"If I fail, I'll start again, there or somewhere else. And if I'm killed, the case is closed."

His luggage had been carried aboard. We shook hands warmly and he went straight to the bar, where he sat alone, reading, nobody to wait on him. On the dock Italian beggar girls were singing, and their song wafted after me as I left, along with the varnishy smell of the recently repainted ship.

Hired by Sun Yat-sen with the title of "legal adviser" at a salary of eight hundred dollars a month; after our

[49]

refusal to supply experts to the Cantonese government, he was assigned to the reorganization and direction of Propaganda (his present position).

When he got to Canton, he heard with keen pleasure that he was indeed in line for eight hundred dollars Mex* each month. But after three months he realized that the payments of both military and civilian salaries in Sun Yat-sen's bureaucracy was highly chancy: they all lived by swindles or "arrangements." By issuing credentials as secret propaganda agents to opium importers, thenceforth sheltered from the various police forces, he made about a hundred thousand gold francs in seven months. Which relieved him of the worry that some unforeseen difficulty would take him by surprise. And Lambert said good-bye to Canton three months later, leaving him in charge of Propaganda, which was only a joke then.

Once free of money worries, Pierre wanted to transform Propaganda from a comic-opera bureau to a powerful weapon. He instituted accurate accounting of the funds granted him and demanded honesty of his subordinates; he had to replace almost all of them. Sun Yat-sen followed these doings with interest, but in spite of his promises the new staff remained unpaid, and for months Pierre spent every day finding ways to pay them. He'd attached the political police to Propaganda; shortly he took control of the city police and the secret police. And with utter indifference to law, he guaranteed Propaganda's survival by undeclared taxes on opium importers, gambling houses, and prostitution. Which is why the police report states:

An energetic man, but without morals.

(*Morals* is delightful.)

* The dollar Mex, or Mexican dollar, was common currency in Chinese cities for years. Roughly two Mexican dollars equaled one U.S. dollar. (Tr.)

[5 0]

Has recruited talented associates, all in the service of the Comintern.

The truth is more complex. He was personally organizing the instrument he'd long dreamed of, and he did all he could to protect it. He knew that if necessary Sun Yat-sen, despite his polite appreciation, wouldn't hesitate to cast him off; and he operated with as little commotion as possible, but implacably. He surrounded himself with young Kuomintang members, clumsy but fanatical, and finally whipped them into shape with the help of a growing number of Russian agents whom famine had driven from Siberia and North China. Before the meeting between Sun Yat-sen and Borodin in Shanghai, the International in Moscow had sounded Pierre, reminding him of his negotiations in Zurich. They found him determined to work for them: he felt that only they commanded the resources needed to create the Cantonese revolutionary organization he wanted, and to replace Chinese subtlety by stubborn drive. He also used what little influence he had with Sun Yat-sen to ease him closer to Russia, and he slipped into a natural collaboration with Borodin when the latter came to Canton.

I gathered from the tone of Pierre's letters that during the first months after Borodin's arrival an important campaign was—finally—in the works; then the letters trailed off, and I was surprised when I heard that the "ridiculous little Cantonese government" had joined battle with England and dreamed of restoring a unified China.

When, after my bankruptcy, Pierre offered me the chance Lambert had offered him six years earlier, all I knew about the battle between Hong Kong and Canton was what I read in the newspapers; and my first orders were given me in Ceylon by a Kuomintang delegate in Colombo during my stopover. It was raining as it rains in the tropics; while I listened to the aged Cantonese, our car zipped along beneath hanging clouds; our streaming wind-shield slapped against dripping palm leaves. I had to make a major effort to persuade myself that the words I was listening to had some connection with reality, with battles, death, agonies. Back aboard, in the bar, still dazed by the old man's speeches, I was curious enough to reread Pierre's last letters. His job—the boss—began to seem real to me. And scattered on my bunk now, in this shiny white cabin, those letters bring back—with my friend's blurred features, with so many clear or confused memories—a great sea whipped by a slanting rain and edged by the long gray line of Ceylon's high plateaus beneath motionless, almost black, clouds. . . .

You know how much I hope you'll come. But don't come if you expect to find that life here fulfills the hopes I had when I left you. The power I dreamed of, and command today, can only be won by a dogged peasant persistence, by unflagging energy, by the constant desire to add to what we already have here just that man, or that element, we need. You may be surprised to read that. Here among my comrades I found the doggedness I lacked, and I believe I've made it mine. I've become strong by putting total absence of scruples at the service of something other than my own interest.

Every day, as we near Canton, I see them put up the bulletins by which he's so forcefully replaced his letters. . . .

This police report is oddly incomplete. At the bottom of the page I see two large exclamation points in blue pencil. Maybe an old note. The information on the second sheet is of another kind altogether:

Keeps Propaganda going these days by taking a percentage of contributions from the overseas Chinese and union dues. Seems to be largely responsible for the un-

deniable enthusiasm here at the idea of a war against the troops we're backing. Thanks to a steady barrage of propaganda, established the closed shop—the importance of which needs no emphasis—when Borodin insisted on it before organizing the strike militia. The seven public and secret police forces have become so many propaganda organizations. Has created an "organ of political instruction," which is a school for speechmakers and propagandists. Has brought the Ministry of Justice (again, no emphasis needed) and the Ministry of Finance under the wing of the Political Bureau, and therefore of the Comintern. Finally, and I emphasize this, he is doing his utmost to promote issuance of the decree (the mere suggestion of which obliged us to request military intervention by the United Kingdom) closing the port of Canton to any ship touching at Hong Kong, a decree which as it has been so rightly said, would destroy Hong Kong as surely as a cancer. *That sentence is posted in several Propaganda offices.*

Beneath that, three lines are underlined twice in red pencil.

Allow me to call your special attention to this: the man is gravely ill. He will be forced to leave the tropics before long.

I'm not so sure.

PART TWO

———

POWERS

Shouts, catcalls, protests, policemen bellowing orders—last night's din begins all over again. This time we're disembarking. We hardly notice Shameen with its tiny tree-shaded houses. Everybody's looking at the nearby bridge, protected by trenches and barbed wire, and mainly at the British and French gunboats even closer, their cannon ranged on Canton. A small motorboat is waiting for Klein and me.

This is the old China, China without Europeans. As if in a canal, the motorboat cuts through yellowish muddy waters between two rows of jam-packed sampans like rude gondolas with wicker roofing. On their bows women, almost all of them old, are cooking over tripods that smell of hot pungent fat; behind many of the women sits a cat, a chicken coop, or a chained monkey. Naked yellow children scamper from one attraction to another, their characteristic bangs flapping like whisks; the children are more graceful and lively than the cats in spite of their round rice-eaters' bellies. The infants sleep, little parcels wrapped in black cloth hung on their mothers' backs. Glowing sunlight plays on the sampans' awnings, accenting the women's shirts and trousers, blue swatches, and the children on the roofs, yellow swatches. Along the waterfront, the irregular skyline of Chinese and American business houses; above, a sky bleached pale by the intense sunlight; and everywhere that same light, fragile as froth, lying on sampans, houses, river, an incandescent fog we knife through.

We dock. A waiting car carries us off at high speed. In an army uniform, the driver bears down permanently on his horn, and the crowd parts as if we were a cow-catcher. I have barely time enough to notice a blue and white multitude to either side—many men in robes—bordered by rows of bamboo blinds embellished by huge black characters; and street vendors trotting, bodies tilted, a shoulder hunched under a bamboo yoke heavily burdened at either end. Briefly alleys flash by, paved with cracked stones, then running into grass fields before some horned edifice or mildewed pagoda. And the staff car of one of the Republic's high officials crosses our path in a great gust, two soldiers, Lugers in hand, standing on the running boards.

Leaving the business section, our car swings onto a tropical boulevard bordered by houses set in gardens, a boulevard without pedestrians, the flat white dazzle of the torrid roadway broken only by the limping figure of a soup vendor who soon vanishes into an alleyway. Klein, who's on his way to Borodin, drops me off in front of a house in colonial style—roof projecting over verandas—surrounded by an iron fence like a chalet outside Paris: this is Garine's house. The iron door is elaborately wrought. I cross a small garden and come to a second door guarded by two Cantonese soldiers in gray uniforms. One takes my card and disappears. While I wait I inspect the other: with his flat cap and the pistol at his belt he reminds me of Czarist officers. But his cap's tilted back on his head and he's wearing espadrilles. The other returns. I may go upstairs.

One flight of narrow stairs, then a spacious room, and through a doorway another room where men are talking loudly. This neighborhood is quiet; I barely hear an occasional far-off auto horn beyond the palm fronds screening two windows; only a straw mat screens the doorway, and

I hear English spoken in the other room. The sentry indicates the mat and goes out.

". . . let Ch'en Chiung-ming organize his army . . ." Beyond the mat an agitated man is talking. "I've been saying so for a month or more! Furthermore Boro's as strong for it as I am! The decree alone, do you understand?"—it's Garine's voice now; a fist hammers a table stressing every word—"the decree alone is enough to destroy Hong Kong! This damned government has got to come out for it! . . . Straw man or not, he's got to march, because we need him! . . . They'll think twice. They know and I know that the decree'll kill their port dead as a . . ."

Footsteps. Men pass in and out.

"What do the committees propose?"

Someone shuffles papers. "Not much." (This is a new voice.) "Most of them, nothing at all, really. Here are two asking for an increase in strike funds and an extension of the unskilled laborers' allocations. This latter also suggests executing the first workers who went back on the job."

"No. Not yet."

"Why not?" Chinese voices, hostile.

"You don't swing death around like a broom."

If anyone came out, I'd look like a spy. Still, I can't blow my nose, or whistle a tune! Let's flip the mat aside and go on in.

Around a desk, Garine in officer's khakis and three young Chinese in white jackets. During the introductions one of the Chinese murmurs, "Some people are afraid to dirty their hands on a broom."

"There were plenty of people who thought Lenin wasn't revolutionary enough," Garine answers, turning quickly, his hand still on my shoulder. Then to me: "Well, you're no younger. You come from Hong Kong?" And without even waiting for an answer, "Yes, you saw Meunier. You have the documents?"

They're in my pocket. I hand them over. At the same moment a sentry comes in carrying a stuffed envelope. Garine passes it to one of the Chinese, who sums it up: "A report from the Kuala Lumpur chapter. It points out their current difficulties raising money."

"And French Indochina?" Garine asks me.

"I have six thousand dollars for you that Gérard collected. He says it's going pretty well."

"Good. Come on." He takes me by the arm and picks up his cap, and we leave. "We're off to Borodin's. It's close by."

We go down the boulevard on deserted sidewalks of scorched grass. The sun plates the white dust with a raw dazzle that almost forces us to shut our eyes. Quickly Garine asks about my trip; then as we walk along he reads Meunier's report, tilting the sheets to reduce the glare. He hasn't aged much, but below the green lining of his cap every feature bears some sign of sickness. His eyes are pouched halfway down his cheeks, his nose is even thinner, the two wrinkles from his nostrils to the corners of his mouth are no more the deep, sharp wrinkles they were; they're wide, loose wrinkles, almost folds, and the flesh seems at once feverish, flaccid, and so weary that when he brightens it stretches and his expression alters completely. About his head as he walks, eyes on the report, the air ripples against the dense greenery and dusty palms, as it always does this time of day. I'd like to talk about his health; but he's finished reading, and rolls the report tight and taps his chin with it as he says, "It's beginning to go sour. There too. The sympathizers are wavering, the house servants are slinking back to their kennels. And here we have to depend on young fools who confuse a revolution with the third act of a Chinese comic opera. We can't divert more money to the strike fund. It's impossible! And anyway it wouldn't change anything. Sick strikes are cured by victories."

"Meunier has no suggestions?"

"He says, in general, morale isn't bad; the weaklings flinch because Britain threatens, by way of the secret police. Otherwise he says, 'Our Chinese committees there propose to kidnap two or three hundred children of the guilty or suspected. They'd bring them here and treat them well but return them only to parents who came looking for them. Obviously, they wouldn't get back to Hong Kong overnight. Everybody's on vacation in the country right now,' he adds. 'It would make the others think.' We won't get very far with that kind of nonsense."

We've arrived. The house is like Garine's, but yellow. As we start in, Garine halts and, in the military manner, salutes an aged Chinese just leaving. The old man extends a hand; we draw nearer. "Monsieur Garine," he says slowly in French, his voice soft, "I came here hoping to run into you. I think a conversation between the two of us would be a good thing. When may I see you?"

"Why, whenever you please, my dear Monsieur Ch'eng-tai. I'll come by and see you to——"

"No, no," he replies, patting the air with one hand as if to calm Garine, "I'll come by, I'll come by. At five, would that suit you?"

"Perfectly. I'll be waiting for you."

As soon as I hear his name, I take a close look. Like the faces of so many old Chinese scholars, his reminds me of a death's-head, because from a distance it seems all jutting cheekbones, dark, hollow eye sockets, an imperceptible nose, and prominent teeth. Closer, his almond eyes are lively and his smile harmonizes with the extreme courtesy of his speech and the distinction of his tone; all of which moderates his homeliness and alters its quality.

He buries his hands deep in his sleeves like a priest and punctuates his conversation with gentle shrugs. For a moment I think of Klein, who also speaks with the whole body; by contrast Ch'eng-tai seems even more delicate, aged, subtle. He's wearing trousers and military tunic of white linen, like almost all Kuomintang leaders. His ricksha, all black—awaits him. Step by tiny step he makes his way to it; his man pulls him away, slowly and carefully; he himself nods gravely, huddled deep into the seat, and seems to be mulling over unspoken arguments. . . .

After watching him off for a' moment, we pass the sentries without identifying ourselves, cross an empty hall, and come to another sentinel, this one in khaki with orange braid. (Is that a mark of distinction?) Behind him is no hanging mat but a closed door.

"Is he alone?" Garine asks; the sentry nods. We knock and enter. The office is spacious. A standing portrait of Sun Yat-sen six feet high bisects the bluish whitewashed wall. Behind a desk covered with all sorts of papers meticulously sorted and separated, Borodin watches us advance, in shadow, a bit surprised (doubtless by my presence) and blinking. He rises and comes toward us, round-shouldered, hand outstretched. Now I can make out the foreshortened face beneath the head of thick wavy hair brushed straight back—all I could see when I first caught sight of him hunched over his desk. He has that look of a shrewd jungle cat so often produced by droopy mustaches, high cheekbones, and eyes like slits. Maybe forty years old.

During his talk with Garine he acts pretty much like a soldier. Garine introduces me, synopsizes—in Russian—Meunier's report, and drops it on the desk; Borodin picks it up and stacks it quickly on a pile of reports held down by another portrait of Sun Yat-sen, this one an etching. He seems struck by one detail and notes it with a few comments. They go on in Russian, their tone lively but worried.

And Garine and I go back to his house for lunch. He walks fretting, eyes downcast.

"Something wrong?"

"Oh, I'm used to it." In front of his house a waiting orderly hands him a report. He reads it as we climb the steps, signs it on the wicker table on the veranda, and returns it. The orderly trots off. Garine seems more and more concerned.

"Well?"

"Well, that's that." His tone is enough.

"Things going badly?"

"Badly. Strikes are fine and dandy but they aren't enough. We need something else now. One particular something: the decree barring Chinese ships from Hong Kong, and foreign ships that want to touch at Canton. The decree's been signed for over a month, but it hasn't been issued yet. The British know the strike can't last forever and they're wondering what we're going to do. Are they betting on Ch'en Chiung-ming? They've sent him arms, military advisers, and money. When the decree was signed, those people in Hong Kong were so scared they cabled England on behalf of every public authority and department, requesting military intervention. The decree's still in the bottom of a drawer somewhere. All right, its enforcement would bring on a war. So what? They can't fight that war! And in the end Hong Kong would be . . ." His fist tightens an imaginary screw. "If we pull just the Cantonese firms out of Hong Kong, we cut port receipts by two-thirds. Ruin."

"Well?"

"Well what?"

"What are you waiting for?"

"Ch'eng-tai. We're not the government yet. That kind

of move will fail if that old fool wants it to fail." He meditates. "Even when you know everything, you only know half the story. I'd love to know—know for sure— if he's involved in whatever T'ang and those second-rate swine are cooking up."

"T'ang?"

"A general like a hundred others. T'ang isn't important. He's working up a coup d'etat. He wants to put us out of business. That's *his* problem. He himself doesn't matter; he's just another risk we have to run. What matters is what we find backing him. Britain for sure, of course. Right now the British have plenty of money for anybody at all who wants to make trouble for us; he's drawing down good money from them for every man in his outfit. And unfortunately Hong Kong's close by, a safe retreat for T'ang and the others when they're beaten. And then there's Ch'eng-tai, the 'honest old Ch'eng-tai' you just saw. I know for sure that if T'ang won—but he won't— he'd offer Ch'eng-tai the top spot, provided T'ang could run things in his name. Ch'eng-tai and only Ch'eng-tai could replace the Committee of Seven. Public organizations and secret societies would both accept him, for sure. And instead of our kind of action he'd publish lovely 'appeals to the peoples of the world' like the one he just issued that Gandhi and Russell supported. Terrific, this Age of Paper! I can see it now: compliments, claptrap, the return of British goods, Englishmen with cigars on the dock, all our work destroyed. All these Chinese cities are like huge jellyfish. We're the backbone here. For how long?"

We're about to sit down to luncheon when another orderly arrives with a message. Garine slits the envelope with a table knife, takes his seat, and reads. "All right. That'll do." The orderly leaves. "The number of crooks hanging around Ch'eng-tai is unbelievable. Day before yesterday a bunch claiming to support him held a meeting. In a kind of plaza not far from the river. He showed up. Dignified and weary, as you saw him a while ago; not to make a speech, of course. And it was something to see, the speechifiers speechifying, standing on tables up above a great square field of not very enthusiastic human heads, against a background of corrugated iron, peaked pagodas, and twisted bits of scrap metal. He kept himself a little way apart, not too far with a large ring of the respectful around him. Some hoodlums attacked him. He had a few Chinese toughs with him who defended him. The chief of police had them all hauled in, attackers and defenders both. And today the number-one defender—this is his interrogation I'm looking at—is asking the interrogating officer for a job, and what's more a job on the police force. Faith is a beautiful thing! And this other paper—here."

He hands it to me. It's a copy of a list drawn up by General T'ang: Garine, Borodin, Nikolaieff, Hong, some Chinese names. *To be shot without delay.*

All during lunch we talk about Ch'eng-tai. Garine thinks of no one else. The adversary. Before he died, Sun Yat-sen said, "Borodin's words are my words." But Ch'eng-tai's words too were his words, and he had no need to say so.

Ch'eng-tai's public life began in Indochina. What had brought him to Cholon? The big town living on the rice trade had nothing to offer the old scholar. He became one of the Kuomintang's organizers there, and more than an organizer, a moving spirit. Whenever the Cochin Chinese government moved against a party member, either on its own or truckling to the rich guilds, Ch'eng-tai popped up. He found work or money for those the government or the police drove into destitution, found ways, and money, to help deportees and their families back into

China. When all hospital doors were closed to party members, he founded a new hospital.

He was president of the Cholon chapter then. Unable to raise the money through dues or contributions, he appealed to the Chinese banks; they turned him down flat. He offered his own holdings in Hong Kong as collateral—two-thirds of his fortune. The banks accepted, and construction began. Three months later, after some devious electioneering, he was ousted as party president; at the same time, the entrepreneurs informed him that because of certain modifications of the estimates, they were obliged to revise costs sharply upward. The banks refused any further loans. Worse yet—pressured by the Cochin Chinese government, which could deport their directors on twenty-four hours' notice, they began to make trouble about the transfer of the previously committed funds. Ch'eng-tai sold off the properties he'd offered as collateral, and the building went up slowly; but no one could say it would ever be finished. In the core of the Kuomintang an underground campaign was waged against him; he suffered grievously but persevered; and while political agitators in white undershirts circulated in Chinese restaurants during the siesta, dropping confidential hints about "his crazy notions" to half-awake artisans dazed by the heat, he put his ancestral home on the block in Canton. Even after the hospital was completed, various bribes still had to be paid; after notifying Grosjean, the antiquarian in Peking, he disposed of his painted scrolls and his famous collection of Sung jade. What was left? Barely enough to let him scrape by. Alone among ranking party members, he doesn't own a car. That's why I saw him rolling off in his ricksha, perhaps rather pleased by a public poverty that rendered his generosity unforgettable.

His nobility is genuine, but shot through with shrewdness. Like Lau-yit, like General Hsü, he's a poet; but he's also the man who made the boycott—originally the defense of a few clever merchants against the Japanese—the accurate weapon we use today. It was he who directed it at the British; he who, knowing Western business ways (raised by the Fathers, he speaks, reads, and writes French and English fluently), skillfully edited Sun Yat-sen's propaganda to lull the British; he who subordinated trade restrictions to the information services, always leaving the British in Hong Kong enough optimism to stockpile goods that the Chinese, at the right moment, suddenly refused to buy.

But his authority is principally moral. Garine says we're not wrong to compare him with Gandhi. His power, though far more limited, is of the same moral order as the Mahatma's. It's above politics, it speaks to the soul, it's not of this world. Both men's power acts to create a myth profoundly disturbing to those of their own race. But if the methods are similar, the men themselves are quite different. At the heart of Gandhi's work is the passionate, consuming desire to teach men how to live. There's nothing of that in Ch'eng-tai; he wants to be neither example nor leader, but adviser. During the most melancholy and troubled hours of Sun Yat-sen's life Ch'eng-tai was at his side, though almost never involved in purely political action; at Sun's death Ch'eng-tai was asked if he would agree to succeed the dictator as president of the party. He refused. He wasn't afraid of the responsibilities, but the role of arbiter seemed nobler, and more suited to his nature, than any other. More: he would not allow himself to assume functions that would fill his life and make him other than what he wanted to be: the caretaker of the revolution. His whole life is a moral protest, and his hope of victory through justice is the most powerful outward manifestation of the ubiquitous, deep, and irremediable frailty of his race.

Possibly that frailty is the only key to his current attitude. Has he truly, passionately wanted all these years to deliver South China from Britain's economic domination? Yes. But in defending and educating an oppressed people whose cause was undeniably just, he grew accustomed to his role by degrees, and came to prefer that role to the victory of those he fought for. Unconsciously, no doubt, but inexorably. He's more loyal to his protest than eager for victory; it suits him to be the soul and symbol of an oppressed people.

He has no children. Not even a daughter. He was once married. His wife died. He married again. Several years later his second wife also died. After his own death no one will perform the yearly rites for him. That imbues him with a steady, gentle pain which he cannot dispel. He's an atheist, or thinks so; but this solitude in life and in death haunts him. He'll bequeath the heritage of his glory to a risen China. Too bad! He was rich and he'll die almost poor, and the glory of his death will be dissipated among millions of men. A final solitude . . . Everybody knows this, and also that the solitude binds him even more closely to the party's fate.

"Noble figure of a victim supervising his own biography," Garine says. Any effort to satisfy personal desires would seem treason to Ch'eng-tai. He's driven now by his character, by the habit of his role, and by age, and he's just about forgotten even the possibility of inferring logical conclusions from his beliefs. It no more occurs to him to mount and direct a decisive battle than the notion of becoming Pope occurs to a devout Catholic. One day Garine ended a discussion of the Third International by saying, "But the Third International *made a revolution.*"

Ch'eng-tai's answer was a gesture at once evasive and dismissive, both hands to his breast, and Garine said he'd never seen the gap between them so clearly.

People think he's capable of action. But he's only capable of one particular kind of action, the kind that requires a man's victory over himself. He succeeded in building a hospital because the obstacles, serious as they were, could always be overcome by selflessness. He was forced to impoverish himself; he did it, and maybe painlessly, proud to think that few men would have. For him, as for Christians, charity is a good work; but where for Christians charity is compassion, for him it's a function of solidarity: only Chinese party members were admitted to his hospital. The grandeur of his life springs from a scorn for the temporal that makes his public accomplishments possible; but even if that scorn is genuine, he knows it's also useful, and Ch'eng-tai, nobly disinterested, has no intention of allowing a selflessness so rare in China to pass unnoticed. That selflessness seemed simply human at first but has become, by a subtle sort of theatrics, his reason for being: he seeks in it the proof of his superiority to other men. His self-abnegation is the outward sign of a pure nonviolent pride, a pride perfectly in accord with his gentle, scholarly nature.

Like every man who sways great masses, this polite little man of polite little gestures is obsessed—obsessed by Justice. He feels that imposing Justice is his private mission; he perceives Justice vaguely as a creation of his own mind; he's obsessed with its defense as others are with sensuality or ambition. He muses only upon Justice; the world exists as a function of, and thanks only to, Justice; it is the highest need of mankind, and also the god who must be satisfied before all others. He trusts it as a child trusts a statue in a pagoda. Long ago his need for it was deep, human, simple; now it possesses him like a fetish.

It may still be his heart's first desire; but it's also a protective divinity without whom nothing may be hazarded, who can't be slighted without the risk of a mysterious revenge. Its grandeur has aged along with him, and all that can be seen of it now is the bloodless corpse. Possessed by the deformed god lurking beneath his gentleness, his smile, and his mandarin's graces, he lives outside this day-to-day revolutionary world Garine says we're all caught up in—lives in a monomaniac's dream among the remnants of an ancient nobility; and that monomania augments his influence and prestige. An intense and confused sense of justice has always been quite strong in China; Ch'eng-tai's life, already passing into legend, and his age have made a symbol of him. The Chinese crave to see him respected just as they crave to see their national character acknowledged. He's temporarily sacred. And the enthusiasm here, whipped up by Propaganda and directed against Britain, can't change direction without losing strength. It's got to carry all before it; but it's still too soon. . . .

During the meal one report after another comes in. Uneasier every minute, Garine takes note of them as soon as they arrive, and stacks them up at the foot of his chair.

The world of old mandarins, opium smugglers, or photographers, of scholars turned bicycle salesmen, of lawyers qualified at the Paris bar, of all sorts of intellectuals hungry for recognition who gravitate to Ch'eng-tai—they all know that only Propaganda and the Comintern delegation are holding the present situation together, sustaining the immense attack that keeps England in check, struggling against the old, failed, unwanted ways, against that republic of bureaucrats whose two pillars were the former mandarins and the new mandarins—doctors, lawyers, engineers. "We're the framework," Garine said a while ago. And from the reports it looks as if everybody's flocked to this General T'ang—probably without Ch'eng-tai's knowledge; he'd frown on a military coup—General T'ang, hardly mentioned in Canton before now, who's their better in one respect at least: courage. These last days T'ang's come into considerable money. There are plenty of British agents among Ch'eng-tai's entourage. When I express surprise that a coup can be mounted without the old man's knowledge, Garine answers, tapping the table, "He doesn't want to know. He doesn't want to lay his moral responsibility on the line. But I don't think he minds suspecting it."

2 P.M.

At Propaganda, with Garine, in the office assigned to me. On the wall, a portrait of Sun Yat-sen, a portrait of Lenin, and two posters in full color. One shows a small Chinese jabbing a bayonet into John Bull's big behind, Bull's hands and feet flying wildly, while a Russian in a fur hat rises over the horizon emitting rays like a sunrise; the other shows a European soldier with a machine gun firing on a crowd of Chinese women and children with their hands up. On the first, 1925 in Arabic numerals and the Chinese character "now"; on the second, 1900 and the character "then." A wide window with a yellow shade down, soaked in sunlight. On the floor, a pile of Chinese newspapers that an orderly comes to take away. The clerks in this branch clip all the political cartoons and file them with summaries of the important articles. On the Louis XVI desk, an overlooked cartoon, doubtless a duplicate: a hand, the fingers labeled Russians, Students, Women, Soldiers, Peasants, and on the palm, Kuomintang. Garine crumples it up and throws it into the wastebasket. (Has he too become tidy?) Against the wall, a cardboard filing cabinet beside the doorway connecting this room to Garine's, his office also full of the soft, rich yellow light that filters through the shades. But there are no posters on his walls; instead of a cardboard filing cabinet, a safe. At the door, a sentry.

Police Commissioner Nikolaieff is sunk in an armchair, his belly bulging, his legs spread. He's obese, and his face has the agreeable look that a pug nose gives to fat blonds. He listens to Garine with his eyes shut and his hands folded on his belly.

"So," Garine says, "have you read the reports sent to you?"

"Up to the minute."

"Good. Is T'ang going to march against us?"

"As soon as he can. Here's a list of the Chinese he wants to arrest. Not to mention yourself."

"Do you think Ch'eng-tai knows?"

"They'd like to make use of him, that's all." The fat man speaks French with a slight accent. His tone—despite his clipped answers you'd think he was chatting with a woman, or was about to add "my dear fellow"—and his calm face and smooth manner make me think of an ancient priest.

"Are a lot of the Secret Police available?"

"Almost all of them."

"Good. Half your men into the city to spread the word that the British are paying T'ang to mount a coup and make Canton a British colony. In the working-class neighborhoods, of course. A quarter of them to the union halls. Your best men. Very important. The rest among the unemployed with copies of the *Canton Gazette* saying that T'ang's friends are demanding an end to strike benefits."

"And the registered unemployed, let me see——"

"Never mind your files: twenty-six thousand."

"All right. We'll have enough men."

"Also some first-rate agents at party meetings tonight, to pass the word that T'ang's about to be struck from the party rolls, that he knows it, and that he's making his bets outside the party. Keep that last vague."

"You're sure we can't just have T'ang arrested?"

"Worse luck."

"Too bad. Time's on his side."

The fat man leaves us, his files under his arm. Garine rings. The orderly brings in a sheaf of visiting cards and spreads them on the table, nipping a cigarette from Garine's open box.

"Show in the union officials."

Seven Chinese file in silently. They wear tunics with Prussian collars and white duck trousers. Young ones, old ones. They stand in a semicircle before the table. One of the oldest is half sitting on the desk: the interpreter. They all listen to Garine:

"There's every chance that a coup will be mounted against us this week. You know as well as I do what General T'ang and his friends stand for. I don't have to remind you how many times our Comrade Borodin had to intervene with the Cabinet to keep the strike pay coming in Canton. In the last analysis you represent your unemployed members, who went all out at the last union meetings to tell all the comrades what good men you are; I know I can count on you. And then here's a list of people in danger from T'ang and Ch'eng-tai and their friends, people who're to be arrested as soon as the coup starts."

He hands them the list. They read, then look at one another.

"You recognize your names? Then when you walk out of this office . . ."

After each sentence the interpreter translates quietly and the others answer in a murmur: litanies.

". . . you cannot go home. Every one of you stay at union headquarters, and sleep there. You three," and he points to three of the Chinese, "your union halls are too far out to be defended. When you leave you're to go fetch your files and bring them back here. I've had offices made ready for you. Each of you give your workers' militia detailed instructions: we have to be able to call up all our men in one hour."

While he was speaking he sent the cigarette box around; it's back in its place. He shuts it with a gentle clack and rises. One after another, as they came in, the Chinese leave, shaking his hand as they pass. He rings.

"Have this one write out the reason for his visit," he says to the orderly, handing him one of the cards. "In the meantime have Lo-Moi come in."

This is a small Chinese with a shaved head and a pimply face, who stands respectfully before Garine, his eyes lowered.

"When we launched the last strikes, here and in Hong Kong, there were too many useless speeches. If the comrades think they're Parliament, they're wrong. And once for all: these speeches have to lead to action. If the boss's house is too far, or not worth working over, they can always lay hands on his car. I repeat, and for the last time: the agitators have got to show what they're attacking. I don't want to have to mention it again."

The small Chinese bows and goes out. The orderly returns with the card Garine gave him, and hands it to him.

"Tanks?" Garine's brows shoot up. "That's Borodin's business." He writes Borodin's address on the card, plus a few words (an introduction, no doubt). Someone knocks twice. "Come in!"

A powerfully built Occidental opens the door. He sports a bushy mustache in the American style and is wearing the same officer khakis as Garine. "Hello, Garine." He speaks French, but it's another Russian.

"Hello, General."

"Well? Has our precious T'ang made up his mind?"

[74]

"You know about it?"

"Most of it. I just saw Boro. The poor boy's sick, he really is! The doctor's worried about a seizure."

"Which doctor, Myroff or the Chinese?"

"Myroff. Now what about T'ang?"

"Two or three days yet."

"He only has his thousand men?"

"And whoever else they can scare up with their money and what the British give them. Altogether fifteen hundred to eighteen hundred. How soon can the red army* be here, at a minimum? Six days?"

"A week. Has Propaganda been working on T'ang's troops?"

"Damn little. They're almost all Honanese and Yunnanese."

"So much the worse. How many machine guns?"

"Twenty-odd."

"You can have five or six hundred cadets in town, Garine, but no more. When the fighting begins, ask me again."

"Let's be sure we have it straight. As soon as T'ang's troops are alerted, you'll send whatever cadets you have, with a machine-gun company and the police bringing up the rear. And we'll attack from the other flank."

"Right."

The man goes out.

"That your chief of staff, Garine?"

"Yes. Galen."

"He looks like a Czarist officer."

"Like all the others."

A new Chinese, white hair in a crew cut. He steps forward, lets the tips of his fingers touch the desk, and waits.

---

* The Cantonese red army.

"You have all your unemployed at the ready?"

"Yes, sir."

"How many could you round up in half an hour?"

"Using what, sir?"

"Using haste. Disregard the transport problem."

"Over ten thousand."

"Good. Thank you."

At which the Chinese with beautiful white hair goes out.

"Who was that?"

"Our paymaster. A scholar. An unfrocked mandarin. A long story." He calls the orderly. "All those still waiting, send them to the police commissioner."

But through the half-open door another Chinese has just come in, perfectly at ease, knocking twice gently as he enters. Fat like Nikolaieff, head shaved, thick lips in a pudding face, he smiles broadly, displaying gold teeth, and cocks a huge cigar between his fingers. He speaks English.

"The boat from Vladivostok in, Monsieur Garine?"

"This morning."

"How much gasoline aboard?"

"Fifteen hundred . . ." (followed by the word for a Chinese unit of measure I'm not familiar with).

"To be delivered when?"

"Tomorrow. The check brought here as usual."

"Do you want me to sign it now?"

"No, no. A time and place for everything."

"Then good-bye, Monsieur Garine. Until tomorrow."

"Until tomorrow." As the Chinese leaves Garine murmurs to me, "He buys up goods that Russia sends us. The Comintern's short of cash these days, and the shipments of matériel keep us going. They do what they can, anyway—gasoline, oil, weapons, instructors. . . ."

He hops up and steps to the door, peers out: nobody

there. He returns to his desk, sits again, and opens a file folder: HONG KONG. The latest reports. Every few moments he hands me certain bits that he wants me to file separately. To cool us off I press the switch on the electric fan: immediately, a blizzard of paper. He stops the fan, sorts the scattered sheets, and goes on underlining odd sentences in red. Reports, reports, reports. While I prepare summaries, he goes out. Reports . . .

The strike paralyzing Hong Kong can't last more than three days longer in its present form.

After their strike pay is cut off, suppose the workers wait ten days before they go back to their jobs; that's thirteen days altogether. So if Borodin hasn't found a new *modus operandi* within two weeks, British ships will drop anchor in the port of Canton. Hong Kong will rise again, and the whole lesson of the strike will have been lost. The blow to Hong Kong has been punishing; the banks have lost enormous amounts, and still do, every day; moreover, the Chinese have seen that Britain isn't invulnerable. But at this juncture our subsidies and those of the British are supporting a city of three hundred thousand where nobody's working. Who'll give up first? We will, inevitably. And over in Wai-ch'ao Ch'en Chiung-ming's army is almost ready to take the field.

We can still bar Canton-bound ships from Hong Kong. But we need a decree for that, and as long as Ch'eng-tai retains his present power, the decree won't be signed.

Hong Kong: England. Behind Ch'en Chiung-ming's army: England. Behind the cloud of grasshoppers surrounding Ch'eng-tai: England.

There are a few books on the desk. The Fathers' Sino-Latin dictionary. Two medical books in English: *Dysentery*, *Malaria*. When Garine comes back, I ask him if it's true that he's not taking care of himself.

"But of course I take care of myself! Of course! I don't always take care of myself too carefully, because I have other things to do, but none of that's very important—to get well I'll have to go back to Europe. I know that. I'll stay there as long as I can. But you don't expect me to leave now!"

I hardly argue: this conversation irritates him. And the orderly has just brought in a letter that Garine's reading intently. He hands it to me, saying only, "The red pencil is Nikolaieff's."

It's a new list, like the one Garine received at lunch, but longer: Borodin, Garine, E. Ch'en, Sun Fo, Liao Chung-k'ai, Nikolaieff, Semyonoff, Hong, a number of Chinese I don't know. Nikolaieff has jotted in the corner, in red, *"Complete list of people to be arrested AND EX-ECUTED ON THE SPOT."* And below he's scrawled hastily, in ink: *"They're having proclamations printed."*

At five the orderly brings in a new card. Garine rises, goes as far as the door, and draws back to let Ch'eng-tai pass. The little old man steps in, takes the armchair, stretches his legs, plunges his hands into his sleeves, and looks at Garine, back behind his desk, with faintly ironic goodwill. But he doesn't speak.

"You want to see me, Monsieur Ch'eng-tai?"

He nods yes, lets his hands emerge from the sleeves, and says in a thin voice, "Yes, Monsieur Garine, yes. I do not believe I need ask if you know of the terrorist attacks these past few days." He speaks quite slowly, carefully, his index finger raised. "I admire your talents too much to suppose that you do not know of them, given the constant communication that your position obliges you to maintain with Monsieur Nikolaieff. Monsieur Garine, these attacks have become too frequent."

Garine answers by a gesture: What can I do about it?

"We understand each other, Monsieur Garine, we understand each other."

"Monsieur Ch'eng-tai, you know General T'ang, do you not?"

"General T'ang is a just and faithful man." And setting his right hand lightly on the desk as if to underline what he says: "I have every hope of persuading the Central Committee to adopt measures against these attacks. I believe it would be well to effect a public indictment of certain men known to us all as the leaders of terrorist groups. Monsieur Garine, I wish to know what would be your reaction, what would be the reaction of your friends, to the proposals I intend to present." He withdraws the hand, slips it back into his sleeve.

"I think we'd all agree, Monsieur Ch'eng-tai," Garine answers, "that for some time now your instructions to your colleagues have been consistently, and rather tiresomely, contrary to our wishes."

"You have been misled, Monsieur Garine. Doubtless you have inexpert advisers, or your intelligence has been misinterpreted. I have issued no instructions."

"Let's say suggestions."

"Not even that. I have made known the drift of my thought, given my opinion, no more." He smiles more and more broadly. "I trust you have no objection to that?"

"I put great stock in your opinions, Monsieur; but I'd be happier—we'd be happier—if the Committee learned about them in another way——"

"—than by its secret police, Monsieur Garine? But I feel as you do. The Committee might, for example, have sent me one of its members, a qualified person. It was certainly possible." He bows slightly. "The proof being that we are here together."

"A few months ago the Committee never felt obliged

to delegate me to discover your opinions; you yourself expressed them openly to us."

"The question is then whether I have changed, or you. I am no longer a young man, Monsieur Garine, and you will perhaps admit that my life——"

"No one would dream of impugning your character; we all respect it, and we all know what China owes you. But..."

Ch'eng-tai has bowed and smiled; hearing "But," he sits up uneasily and gazes at Garine.

"But you in turn don't deny the value of our work. And yet you try to thwart us."

Ch'eng-tai says nothing, hoping that the silence will disquiet Garine and keep him talking. After a moment he changes his mind: "Perhaps it is indeed desirable that we clarify our situation. The abilities of certain Committee members, and your own in particular, Monsieur Garine, are notable. But you generate powerful support for a spirit which it is impossible for us to approve fully. How important do you consider the Whampoa Military Academy?" He spreads his hands like a Catholic priest deploring the sins of his flock. "I cannot be accused of clinging too closely to the old Chinese ways; I have contributed to their destruction. But I believe, I believe firmly, I will even say I live by the conviction, that the party's actions will not be worthy of what we expect of it, unless they are founded in justice. Do you wish to contradict that?" And in an even softer voice: "No. Let the imperialists accept their responsibilities. A few more massacres of miserable victims will do more for the cause than all the cadets in Whampoa."

"You hold their lives cheap."

Ch'eng-tai raises his head to stare at Garine: it gives him the look of an old Chinese teacher outraged by a student's question. I think he's angry, but nothing of it shows. His hands are still in his sleeves. Is he thinking of the massacre at Shameen? Finally he speaks, as if stating firm conclusions: "Oh, less than if we sent them to be shot down by the volunteers in Hong Kong, don't you think?"

"But that's never been suggested. You know as well as I do that there'll be no war, that England can't fight a war here! Every day shows the Chinese people—and the party does its share—the foolishness of the Europeans' bluff, the futility of power based on rusted bayonets and muzzled cannon."

"I am not so sure of that. War would not displease you. It would impress us all with your talents, which are remarkable, with Monsieur Borodin's organizing skills, and with General Galen's martial qualities." (What a note of covert scorn on that word *martial!*)

"But isn't the liberation of all China a noble and just thing?"

"You are truly eloquent, Monsieur Garine. But we do not see this in the same light. You like experiments. In conducting them you employ—how shall I say this?—whatever means are required. In the present case, the people of this city. Shall I be honest with you? I would prefer that they not be employed at that task. I love to read tragic tales, and I can admire them; I do not love seeing them unfold in my own family. If I dared express my thoughts in too violent a manner, which would exaggerate them, and use an expression you sometimes use in regard to another process altogether, I might say that I cannot without sorrow see my countrymen turned into guinea pigs."

"It seems to me that if any country has been experimented on by the whole world, it's not China but Russia."

"No doubt, no doubt. But perhaps Russia *needed* that. You feel that need. You and your friends. Certainly you would not flee at the moment of danger." He bows. "Which is not, in my view, Monsieur Garine, sufficient reason to go out looking for it. I want—I wish devoutly—to see Chinese tried by Chinese courts everywhere in China, truly protected by Chinese police, possessing truly and not merely in principle a land of which they are the legitimate masters. But we have no right to attack Britain overtly by governmental action. We are not at war. China is China, and the rest of the world is the rest of the world."

Ruffled, Garine does not answer immediately.

Ch'eng-tai goes on: "I know only too well where that attack would lead us. I know only too well that it would reinforce the fanaticism that came among us with you."

Garine meets his gaze.

"A fanaticism the value of which I do not deny, but which I cannot accept, to my regret, Monsieur Garine. We must build on truth alone." He spreads his hands as if apologizing.

"And do you believe, Monsieur Ch'eng-tai, that Britain cares as much for justice as you do?"

"No. And that is why in the end we shall vanquish them. Without violence and without combat. Before five years have passed, no British products will be able to enter China."

He's thinking of Gandhi. Garine, tapping the table with the butt of his pencil, answers slowly, "If Gandhi hadn't stepped in—he too in the name of justice—to break the last Hartal, the British would be out of India."*

"If Gandhi had not stepped in, Monsieur Garine, India, which is teaching the world the most important lesson it can learn today, would only be an Asian country in revolt."

*Hartal: a day of national mourning when business is suspended, used as a form of boycott or general strike. (Tr.)

"We're not here to provide glowing examples of defeat!"

"Let me thank you for a comparison which honors me more than you can possibly believe, but of which I am unworthy. By his own suffering Gandhi redeemed his countrymen's mistakes."

"And by the floggings his virtue brings down on them."

"You are angry, Monsieur Garine. But why? China will choose between your ideas and mine."

"But it's for us to make China what she ought to be! And how can we do it if you and I can't agree, if you teach her contempt for what she needs most, if you won't even admit that the first requirement is to *exist!*"

"China has always conquered her conquerors. Slowly, it is true. But always. Monsieur Garine, if China is to become something other than the China of Justice, the China I have—modestly—struggled to build; if she is to become like . . ."

(A pause. Understood: Russia.)

". . . I see no need for her to exist. Let her remain a great memory. Despite all the abuses of the Manchu dynasty, the history of China commands respect."

"And do you think the pages we're writing today represent a falling-off?"

"Fifty centuries of history must comprise a few very sad pages, Monsieur Garine, some doubtless sadder even than those of which you speak; but at least it is not I who wrote them."

He rises with some difficulty and proceeds to the door with his tiny steps. Garine escorts him. As soon as the door closes, he turns to me: "Dear God, deliver us from saints!"

Latest reports: T'ang's officers are in the city. But there's nothing to worry about tonight.

"Even in the world of ideas, or rather emotions,"

Garine explains at dinner, "we're not powerless against Ch'eng-tai. All modern Asia is learning about individual life and discovering death. The masses are understanding that their poverty is hopeless and they can't expect anything from an afterlife. The lepers who stopped believing in God poisoned the fountains. Every man who's cut himself off from Chinese life, from its rituals and hazy beliefs, and then rebels against Christianity, is a good revolutionary. You'll see a perfect example of that in Hong, and almost all the terrorists you meet. Simultaneously with the fear of a meaningless death, a death that redeems nothing and avenges nothing, another idea is born: the possibility that any man can beat the life of mass misery and struggle through to a particular, individual life; they think of it vaguely as well-being, worth much more than wealth.

"Borodin and some of his Russian methods can thank that notion for a good deal of their success; the idea provokes the workers to demand elected supervisory committees in their factories—not out of vanity but to give themselves the feeling of a more truly human existence. Isn't it something like that, the idea of possessing an individual life, distinct from all others in God's eyes, that makes Christianity so strong? And every day I see how small a step it is between those impulses and hatred; even fanatical hatred. If you show a coolie the boss's car, he can react in various ways; but if he has his legs broken . . . and there are a lot of legs broken in China. The hardest thing is to convert Chinese subtlety into nerve. You have to nurture their self-confidence slowly, so it doesn't dissipate after a few days; show them victories, plenty of them, one after another, before sending them into battle. The struggle against Hong Kong is excellent for that, even if we launched it for a variety of reasons. The results have been brilliant and we're making them even more brilliant.

They see ruin hanging over a symbolic England, and they all want to be in at the kill. They see themselves conquerors, and conquerors without having to put up with the militarism they hate because it reminds them of defeats. For them as for us, today it's Hong Kong, tomorrow Hankow, day after tomorrow Shanghai, later Peking. The momentum generated by that struggle has to sustain —it will sustain!—our army against Ch'en Chiung-ming's, and later on the drive north. That's why we've got to win, why we've got to use any means at all to keep this popular enthusiasm—it's becoming a historic force—from being frittered away in the name of justice and other such fairy tales."

"So much strength so easily destroyed?"

"Destroyed, no. Brought to nothing, yes. All it took was one badly timed sermon from Gandhi—because the Indians had liquidated a few English, for God's sake!— to break the last Hartal. Enthusiasm can't survive hesitation, particularly here. What you need is to have every man feel that his whole life's bound up in the revolution, that it'll lose all its value if we're beaten." After a pause he adds, "You also need a tough-minded minority."

After dinner he goes to ask after Borodin. The fever the doctors worried about has hit him, and the International's representative, confined to his bed, can neither read nor discuss anything whatever. Garine too worries about the fever, and his worries lead us to talk about himself for a moment. To one of my questions he answers, "There are plenty of old hatreds deep inside me that had a lot to do with making me a revolutionary."

"But you've never been poor."

"Oh, that has nothing to do with it. My deepest hostilities aren't so much against possessors as against the stupid principles they spout to defend their possessions. And there's another thing: when I was an adolescent I thought in generalities, and I didn't need anything concrete to confirm me in my self-confidence. I still have self-confidence, but with a difference: today I need *proof.* What ties me to the Kuomintang—"

And he sets his hand on my arm: "—is habit, but most of all the need for a common victory."

THE NEXT DAY

Terrorist operations are always violent. Yesterday a rich businessman, a judge, and two former magistrates were assassinated, some in the street and some in their homes.

Tomorrow Ch'eng-tai will ask the Executive Committee to have Hong and all other suspected heads of anarchist and terrorist groups arrested.

THE NEXT DAY

"T'ang's troops are moving up."

We've just started lunch. We leave immediately. The car races along beside the river. We see nothing yet in the city. But inside the houses we stop at, machine-gun squads are ready. As soon as we've passed, the regular dock police and the strike militia clear away the crowds and halt all traffic on the bridges, near which the machine gunners set up. T'ang's troops are across the river.

Outside Garine's office at Propaganda, Nikolaieff is waiting for us with a rumpled, rather handsome young Chinese: Hong, head of the terrorists. Not until I hear his name do I notice the length of his arms, the somewhat simian length Gérard spoke of. Already the corridor's full of agents: they were staked out near the homes of our friends on T'ang's list, and it was their job to notify us as soon as T'ang's arrest patrols showed up. They tell us they've just seen soldiers force their way into the houses, enraged at missing their victims, and carry off women, servants. . . . Garine shuts them up. Then he asks each of them where he was posted, and marks the raided houses on a map of Canton.

"Nikolaieff."

"Yes."

"Go on down. A message to Galen. Take it yourself. Then, an agent by car to every headquarters: each union to send out fifty volunteers against each patrol. The patrols will head back toward the river. Volunteers to the river-bank. Two squads of cadets in charge, with a machine gun apiece."

Nikolaieff rushes off, already short of breath, his fat body bobbling. There's a mob of agents in the corridor now; a Cantonese officer and a tall European (Klein, I think, but he's in shadow) interrogate them quickly before passing them along to Garine. Another Cantonese officer, very young, shoulders his way through the white-suited, white-gowned crowd. "Permission to leave, Commissar?"

"Granted, Colonel. You'll pick up messages at bridge number three." Garine hands him a map with the location of patrols marked in red, and T'ang's starting point and possible routes. The river slashes blue through the city: the battle will be fought there, as always in Canton. I remember Galen's remark: "Pincers. If they don't get past the bridges, they're finished."

A young clerk rushes up with messages.

"Hold on, Colonel! Here's a note from the police: T'ang has fourteen hundred men."

"I have only five hundred."

"Galen told me six."

"Five. You have lookouts all along the river?"

"Yes. No danger of having your flanks turned."

"Good enough. We'll hold the bridges." The officer makes off without another word. Over the tumult we

[87]

hear the squeal of his car starting up and the ceaseless horn fading as he drives off. It's hot, hot. We're all in shirt sleeves; our jackets are heaped up in a corner.

Another note, a copy of one of T'ang's. "Objectives: banks, railway station, post office," Garine reads aloud. He reads on in silence, then speaks again: "They've got to cross the river first."

"Garine! Garine! Feng Lia-dong's troops—" It's Nikolaieff come back, sponging his broad face with his kerchief, his hair damp, his eyes rolling like marbles. "They've gone over to T'ang! The Whampoa roads are cut."

"Sure?"

"Sure." And in a lower voice, "We'll never hold them alone."

Garine studies the map spread on the table. Then he shrugs nervously and goes to the window. "Not much choice." He shouts: "Klein!" More quietly: "Hong, get over to the drivers' hall and bring back about fifty men." Turning again to Nikolaieff: "Telephone? Telegraph?"

"Cut, of course."

Klein comes in. "What?"

"Feng's ratted on us and cut off Whampoa. Take a patrol of red guards and agents. Requisition—and fast— anything you see in the way of cars. Stick a driver and an agent in each one. You'll find the drivers downstairs, Hong's gone to round them up. Have them drive all over town—but not cross the bridges—and send me as many unemployed and strikers as they can. Check the halls. Have the stewards send us all the men they can spare. And find a way to get to the Colonel and tell him to give you a hundred cadets."

"He'll holler."

"No choice, you fool! Bring them back yourself."

Klein leaves. In the distance faint gunfire crackles.

"Now if we just don't get bottled up! If we can round up three thousand to start with . . ." He calls the cadet who was screening agents with Klein: "Send a messenger to the seamen's union hall. Thirty coolies right away."

Another car squeals off. I glance out the window: a dozen cars and drivers wait outside the building. Each departing messenger takes one; squealing, the car emerges from the great slanting shadow of the building and disappears in a cloud of sun-shot dust. No gunfire now. I hear a man say to Garine behind me, "Three patrols captured. The three messengers from our units are waiting."

"Shoot the officers. The men . . . where are they?"

"At the union halls."

"Good. Disarm them. Handcuffs. If T'ang forces the bridges, shoot them."

As I turn the speaker leaves, but he comes back immediately: "They say they have no handcuffs."

"God damn it!" The private telephone rings. "Hello! Captain Kovak? Propaganda commisar, yes. Burning? How many houses? The other side of the river? Let 'em burn." He hangs up. "Nikolaieff. What kind of guard around Borodin's house?"

"Forty men."

"It'll do for now. Is there a stretcher handy?"

"I had one taken in a while ago."

"Good." He too glances out the window, clenches his fists, and speaks to Nikolaieff again: "They're already screwing things up. Go downstairs. First, the cars in single file. Then a road block, and the unemployed in close ranks." Downstairs like a shot Nikolaieff scurries, waving his arms, foreshortened, his face hidden beneath his white helmet. With a tremendous roar the cars back around, make room, line up. In the shade wait two or three hundred men in rags, almost all of them squatting. More troop in every minute. Confused, dazed, they question the others, then

[89]

squat behind them, also seeking shade. Behind me I hear, "Bridges one and three have been attacked."

"Were you there?"

"Yes, Commissar, at number three."

"Well?"

"They couldn't break through the machine guns. They're filling sandbags now."

"Good."

"The Colonel gave me this note for you."

I hear the envelope torn open.

"More men? Yes, yes," Garine says angrily. Then in a mutter, "He's afraid they won't hold."

Outside, the ragged crowd is swelling. On the shady borderline fights break out. "Garine, there must be five hundred men down there."

"Still nobody from the seamen's hall?"

The clerk says, "Nobody, Commissar!"

"Too damn bad." He raises the shade and shouts out the window, "Nikolaieff!"

The fat man lifts his face into the light and comes toward the window.

Garine reaches into a desk drawer and throws him a package of armbands. "Take thirty men, stick an armband on them, and start passing out weapons." He turns back.

We hear Nikolaieff's voice below: "The keys, for God's sake!"

Garine detaches a small key from a large bunch and tosses it out the window; the fat man catches it in cupped hands. Far down the road, stretcher bearers come into sight carrying wounded. "Two red guards at the end of the street, for God's sake! No wounded here just now!"

Wearied by the dazzle of sunlight on the dusty streets and walls, I turn back. Everything swirls, blurred. The propaganda posters on the wall are patches of color, Garine pacing up and down is a blob. . . . Quickly my eyes adjust to the shade. The posters spring to life. Garine comes back to the window. "Nikolaieff! Rifles only!"

"All right."

Swarming thicker every minute, hemmed in by uniformed police and one strike militiaman doubtless sent by Klein, the mob of unemployed surges toward the door: the rifles are in the basement. A huge crowd, still sheltered in shadow. In formation and led by a clerk, twenty-odd men with armbands march into the sunny area. "Garine, some new men with armbands."

He looks. "Coolies from the seamen's hall. Good."

Silence then. While we wait for something to happen, the heat saps us. Down below, confused noises: murmurs, clogs, uneasiness, a street vendor's cricket, the shouts of a soldier shooing him off. Outside the window, dazzle and glare. A hush full of suspense. A rhythmic tramp, sharper, clearer, as marching men approach; a sharp clack as they halt. Silence. Murmurs. A lone man coming upstairs. The clerk. "The coolies from the seamen's hall are here, Commissar."

Garine writes, and folds the sheet of paper.

The clerk extends a hand for it.

"No!" Garine crumples the paper and tosses it into a basket. "I'll go myself."

But here come more clerks waving messages. He reads. "Later for Hong Kong," and he flings the reports into a drawer.

A cadet comes in. "Commissar, the Colonel needs men."

We look out the window again. Now the crowd stretches to the end of the street—its limit the line of shade —rippling with movement ceaselessly absorbed, like the motion of the sea. "At least fifteen hundred."

The clerk is still waiting. Garine writes again, and this time hands him the orders.

The private phone rings again. "What rioters? Good God! . . . You're supposed to know that! . . . Well all right, how did they get there? . . . Several banks? Good. Let 'em attack." He hangs up and starts out of the room.

"Shall I follow you?"

"Yes," he says, in the corridor.

We go on downstairs. Men with armbands, just assigned by Nikolaieff, are lugging rifles up from the basement. From the stoop their comrades distribute the weapons to the unemployed, almost in regular ranks now. But the coolies from the seamen's union have hauled up cases of ammunition, and the armed men are jammed in with others trying to break through and pick up ammunition before they've been issued rifles.

Garine shouts in bad Chinese; nobody hears him. He leaps to the open crate and sits on it. The distribution of weapons comes to a halt. The surge ebbs. From the rear ranks, cries and questions.

He orders the unarmed men to fall back quickly and the armed men to step forward; three by three—it's exasperatingly slow—these pass by the crate and pick up their cartridges. In the basement coolies are opening more crates: the bang and tap of hammers and chisels. And the sound of marching men approaches, like a few minutes ago. Because of the crowd we can't see a thing. Garine jumps onto the stoop for a look: "The cadets!"

He's right. It's the cadets, led by Klein. Panting coolies come out of the basement, shoulders bruised by the broad bamboo poles fresh crates of ammunition dangle from. Klein reaches us.

"Two cadets to help you," Garine tells him. "Everybody who has ammunition, twenty paces forward. Men with rifles and no ammo, ten paces. In between, a crate and three men to pass it out."

And when all that's done, without commotion, in a

thick cloud of sunlit dust, "Now. Rifles first, ammo three paces farther. Cadets all the way up front. Fall the men in by tens. One leader for each squad, a strike militiaman if possible—if not, the first man in line. Each cadet take a hundred fifty men and double-time to the river for the Colonel's orders."

We go back upstairs, and again the first thing we do is look out the window. The street's mobbed now. In sun as in shade, organizers perched on men's shoulders are shouting at the crowd. We hear distant machine-gun fire. Below, a first fully armed company trots off under a cadet's orders.

And helpless, passive waiting begins, tension fraying every frustrated nerve. Waiting. Nothing. Below the window, companies form one by one and move out, double time. Reports about Hong Kong are brought in. Garine throws them into a drawer. We keep hearing the machine guns, like the sound of torn cloth, and now and then the isolated crack of a rifle; but all that seems far away, merging with the terrorist bombs we heard yesterday.

We still hold the bridges. Five times T'ang's troops have tried to force them, but never got past our machine-gun fire at the bridgeheads. Each time, a cadet brings a dispatch: "ATTACK BRIDGE NO.—— BEATEN BACK." And again we wait, Gairne pacing up and down his office or covering his blotter with dense, rococo doodles; myself looking out the same window at the same muster. Two spies have swum the river to come in and report: across the bridges, pillage and arson. Hanging above the street, a very faint smoke softens the dazzle of the very calm sky.

Garine and I race toward the river by car. Nobody in the streets. The fancy shops' iron shutters are closed, the smaller shops are boarded up. As we pass, faces appear at windows behind a hanging cloth or a bed on end, and disappear quickly. An old woman with bound feet, running with a baby in her arms and a baby on her back, vanishes around a corner.

We stop a few yards from the river, at a parallel street, to avoid enemy fire from the far bank. The Colonel has set up headquarters in a house not far from the main bridge. In the courtyard, officers and children. On the second floor, a map of Canton spread out on a table; at the window three wooden beds on end leave only a tiny loophole: a ray of sunlight peeks in and makes a pointed stain on the Colonel's knee.

"Well?"

The Colonel asks, "Have you seen this?" and hands him a note.

The note's in Chinese. Garine and I read it together. He seems to understand it pretty well. All the same, I translate quietly: General Galen is attacking Feng's troops, which separate our two wings, and is marching on the city; Commandant* Chiang Kai-shek is on the march with his best machine-gun squads to take T'ang's troops from the rear.

"No. It must have come in since I left. You're sure you can hold out here?"

"Of course."

"Galen's going to scatter Feng like a rooster on a dung-heap. With his firepower it's a cinch. Do you think Feng's troops will fall back on the city?"

"Probably."

"Good. You have enough men?"

"More than I need."

"Can you give me ten machine guns and a captain?"

The Colonel reads several dispatches. "Yes."

"I'm going to barricade the streets and set up machine-

* Of the military academy.

[94]

gun nests at the approaches. If the retreating troops fall back this way, we'll send 'em looking for greener pastures."

"You sure will." The Colonel snaps an order at his aide-de-camp, who moves out at a trot. We leave; the tiny ray of sunlight pricks us each in turn. Outside, the shooting has died down.

Twenty cadets are waiting for us, clinging to two cars like flies, squeezed into jury-rigged seats on the fenders, sitting on the hood, standing on the running boards. The captain joins us in our car. The cars start up and gather speed, jouncing the cadets at every pothole.

On his desk new dispatches await Garine. He hardly looks at them. He gives the captain command of the new companies still forming. With the sun westering, the whole street is in shade; it's solid with men's heads.

"Requisition whatever you need for the barricades!"

Leaving Nikolaieff to form and arm the companies, Klein goes down to the basement again with twenty cadets trooping after him. They reappear in the corridor, a blurry bunch, only the glitter of reflections sharp on their machine-gun barrels. And again cars take off in a clash of gears and blare of horns, overloaded with bouncing soldiers and leaving flotsam in their wake—khaki caps.

Two hours of waiting. Every little while another dispatch. One alert: toward four o'clock the enemy carried the second bridge. But the reserves of armed workers along the riverbank closed quickly with T'ang's troops, and held, and gave our mobile machine-gun company time to move in and retake the bridge. Then in the alleyways parallel to the quay they shot prisoners.

Around five-thirty the first of Feng's fleeing men show up. Greeted by machine-gun fire, they look for greener pastures.

We inspect our posts. The car stops not too near. Garine, a Cantonese clerk, and I proceed on foot to the ends of streets blocked, the view cut off, by low barricades improvised of beams and beds. Behind them machine gunners are smoking long local cigars and keeping an eye peeled, through loopholes. Garine observes in silence. A hundred yards from the barricades, the workers we've armed are waiting; they squat, they chatter, they listen to speeches by their temporary noncoms, strike militia with armbands.

And when we go back to Propaganda, the waiting begins again. But it's not such a nervous wait. At the last outpost we inspected, a runner brought Garine a message from Klein: Commandant Chiang Kai-shek has forced T'ang's roadblocks, and T'ang's troops have dispersed and headed for the hills. The firing's ended near the bridges but goes on, sustained and heavy, like a distant hailstorm, on the far bank; sometimes we hear grenades go off like enormous firecrackers. The battle recedes quickly into the distance, as quickly as night falls. While I eat dinner in Nikolaieff's office, sorting the last dispatches from Hong Kong, streetlights wink on; and in full night all I hear is an occasional isolated, lonely burst.

When I go back down to the second floor, I hear voices and the clack of weapons in the dark street. Near the cars, in triangular patches of headlight, stand the dark shapes of cadets, striped by gleaming bars of light: their weapons. One of Chiang Kai-shek's battalions is already in the street. Nothing's visible outside the glaring beams of light, but I can sense the lively motion of a crowd in the shadows, and their odd urge to raise their voices, an urge that always follows a battle.

Seated at his desk, Garine's eating a tremendous breadstick that crackles as he chews, and talking to General Galen, who paces the room.

"I can't draw any firm conclusions right now. From the reports I've already seen I can say this much: there are pockets of resistance everywhere, and another attempt like T'ang's is still possible."

"Was T'ang captured?"

"No."

"Dead?"

"I don't know yet. But if it's T'ang today, it's somebody else tomorrow. Money from England's always there, and from Chinese tycoons too. You fight or you don't fight. But—" He stands up, blows the desk top clean, shakes the bread crumbs out of his clothes, steps to the safe, opens it, and takes out a pamphlet that he hands to Galen. "This is what really matters."

"That old bastard!"

"No. He doesn't know a thing about these pamphlets."

I look over Galen's shoulder. The pamphlet announces the formation of a new government, and the offer of its presidency to Ch'eng-tai. "They know they can make an opposition with him. All our propaganda has to buck his influence."

"How long have you had this?"

"An hour."

"His influence. Yes. He's the magnet. Don't you think it's gone on long enough?"

Garine considers. "It's hard to figure. Even harder because I'm beginning to mistrust Hong. He's ordering executions on his own—of people who've made large contributions to the party."

"Replace him."

"Have to think about that. He has a lot of talent, and it's a bad time. And if he stops being with us, he'll be against us."

"So what?"

"He can't do any permanent damage; terrorists are always reckless and badly organized. But for a few days..."

"Naturally!" Garine says when he walks into his office this morning and sees the stacks of reports. "It's always like this after a crisis." And we go to work. The reports we sort are dead scraps of paper, but they describe lively action. The motives and desires behind yesterday's doings, and the day before; the violence of men about whom all I know is that they're dead or on the run; and the hopes of other men, who'll try to do tomorrow what T'ang couldn't do today.

Garine works in silence, assembling all the documents— and there are plenty—that relate to Ch'eng-tai. Sometimes as he plucks out a sheet or marks it in red pencil, he says "Again" under his breath. All our enemies converge in that old man. T'ang, who thought he'd force the bridges fast enough to capture the weapons stored at Propaganda, wanted to make him president in a new government. Men who hate or fear action, men who live by yearnings and regrets, men who flock around the leaders of secret political societies, old men who once worked with Ch'eng-tai: his life imposes order and direction on the whole moiling mass of them.

And now the dispatches from Hong Kong. T'ang made his way back to the city. Britain knows that Propaganda's short of money, and has taken heart again. Even better than when I was actually in Hong Kong, I understand this new kind of warfare, with cannons replaced by slogans, with defeated cities not sacked and burned but occupied by the great silence of an Asian strike, by the uneasy emptiness of deserted towns where furtive figures vanish in the muted clack of clogs. Victory lies not in the name of a

[9 8]

battle but in charts and graphs, in reports, a drop in housing costs, demands for subsidies, the flowering of white plaques that gradually replace the trade names of great foreign firms in Hong Kong's doorways. . . . The other kind of war, the old kind, is in the works too: Ch'en Chiung-ming's army is training under British officers.

"Every report says 'Money, money, money!' We'll be forced to cut off strike pay." And on each request Garine nervously doodles a capital D: the decree. A number of Cantonese firms that the decree would ruin forever—they once offered Borodin considerable sums—have turned to Ch'eng-tai's friends.

Around eleven o'clock, Garine goes out. "We've got to shake that decree loose. If Galen comes in, tell him I've gone to see Ch'eng-tai."

I go on working, with Nikolaieff. Our chief of police is a former Okhrana agent—Borodin knows his record— now with the Cheka.* He infiltrated terrorist organizations before the war and had a number of militants arrested. His information was the best, because he supplemented his own tips and reports with his wife's, she being a sincere and respected terrorist whose subsequent death was a strange story. His comrades slowly stopped trusting him for various small reasons but without enough evidence or inner conviction to justify executing him. The Okhrana marked him useless and stopped his pay. He couldn't work. He fell from humiliation to humiliation, was a tourist guide, a dealer in pornography. Now and then, desperate, he appealed to the police, who sent him small change for old time's sake; he lived on, disheartened, going to pot, yet linked to the police by an odd esprit de corps.

* The Okhrana was the Czarist secret police; the Cheka was the early Soviet secret police and was actually superseded in 1922 by the OGPU. (Tr.)

In 1914, begging for fifty rubles—it was his last request—he turned in his neighbor, an old woman who was caching weapons, as if to discharge the debt.

The war saved him. He decamped from the front in 1917, found himself stranded in Vladivostok and then Tientsin, where he shipped as a dishwasher on a coaster headed for Canton. Here he took up his old profession of informer, displaying such talent that four years later Sun Yat-sen gave him an important post in the secret police. The Russians seem to have forgotten his early career.

While I sort the mail from Hong Kong, he analyzes the failure of yesterday's uprising. "You understand, young fellow, I picked out the biggest hall. A big one, very big. So, I sit in the presidential armchair, alone, all alone on-stage; all alone, you understand? Just a clerk in a corner and six red guards behind me who speak only Cantonese. Pistols in hand, of course. Most of the time when the guy comes in he clicks his heels (there's still brave men, like your buddy Garine says), but he never clicks his heels on the way out. If the place was full of people, an audience, I wouldn't get a thing out of them. The prisoners'd hold out. But when we're alone . . . You can't understand about that: all alone." And with a flabby smile, the smile of a fat old man excited by a nude little girl, he adds, crinkling his eyelids: "If you knew what cowards they turn into . . ."

When I go home for lunch I find Garine scribbling away. "Just a second, I'm almost finished. I have to set it down right away or I'll forget it. It's my visit to Ch'eng-tai."

After a few minutes I hear the sound of a pen striking a long dash. He shoves the papers away. "It seems his last house is sold. He's boarding with a poor photographer, and that must be why he wanted to come to me, the other day. They show me into the studio, a little room all in shadow. He sets out the armchair for me and takes the divan. Somewhere in a courtyard a lantern merchant's hammering on tin—so we have to raise our voices. Anyway, you can read it all." He hands me the sheaf of paper. "Beginning with 'But doubtless.' C is him, G is me, obviously. No, no, I'm going to read it to you. You wouldn't understand the abbreviated notes." He glances down but before reading adds, "I'll spare you the useless honorifics at the beginning. Mandarin and distinguished as usual. When I backed him against the wall and asked him straight if he'd vote for the decree, aye or nay, he said, 'Monsieur Garine' "—Garine does a passable imitation of the old man's frail, singsong, slightly professorial voice— " 'Monsieur Garine, will you be kind enough to allow me to ask you a few questions? I know it is not the customary thing... '

" 'Please do.'

" 'I should like to know if you remember the time when we founded the military academy.'

" 'Quite well.'

" 'In that case it is possible that you have not forgotten that when you were kind enough to seek me out, to acquaint me with your project, you said to me—you affirmed to me—that the school was to be established so that Kuang-tung might defend itself.'*

" 'And?'

" 'To defend itself. You will perhaps recall that with you, and with the young commandant Chiang Kai-shek, I visited several noted personalities. I even went alone at

* Kuang-tung is the province of which Canton is the major city. It was at this time relatively autonomous. (Tr.)

times. Public speakers insulted me, and termed me a mili-
tarist. Me! I know that a life of honor inevitably draws
insults, and I scorn them. But I stated to men worthy of
respect, of consideration, men who reposed confidence in
me: "You want to be sure that I am a man of justice. I
ask you to send your child, your son, to that academy. I
ask you to forget what the wisdom of our ancestors has
taught us: the infamy of the military career." Monsieur
Garine, did I or did I not say that?'

" 'But who would question it?'

" 'Well then. One hundred and twenty of those children are dead. Three of them were only sons. Monsieur
Garine, who is responsible for those deaths? I am.'

"His hands in his sleeves, he bows deeply and rises
saying, 'I am an aged man, and have long since forgotten
the hopes of my youth—a time when you were not born,
Monsieur Garine. I know what death is. I know that
some sacrifices are necessary. . . . Of those young men,
three were only sons—only sons, Monsieur Garine—and
I have seen the fathers since. Every young officer who does
not die in defense of his province, dies in vain. And I
advised that death.'

" 'Those are splendid arguments; I'm sorry you didn't
lay them before General T'ang.'

" 'General T'ang knows them, and has forgotten them
like others. . . . Monsieur Garine, factions and splinter
groups mean nothing to me. But as the Committee of
Seven—a segment of the people—places some value on
my thinking, I shall not withhold it from them.' Very
slowly he adds, 'Whatever the danger to myself. Please
believe that I am sorry to speak to you in this manner.
You have compelled me to. I regret it, truly. Monsieur
Garine, I shall not support your proposal. I shall doubtless go so far as to oppose it. I believe that you and your
friends are not good shepherds to my people—' "

In his ordinary voice Garine reminds me, "It was the Fathers who taught him French."

" '—and even that you represent a danger to them. I believe that you are extremely dangerous, for you do not love them.'

" 'And whom should the infant prefer, the wet nurse who loves him and lets him drown, or the one who does not love him but knows how to swim and saves him?'

"He thinks it over awhile, cocks his head back to look at me and answers respectfully. 'That will perhaps depend, Monsieur Garine, on what the child has in his pockets.'

" 'Good Lord, you ought to know that; you've been supporting him for almost twenty years and you're still poor.'

" 'I never sought——'

" 'Unlike myself! You can look at my shoes, worn right through'—I leaned against the wall and showed him one of my soles—'and see how rich corruption's made me.'

"That upsets him but it's silly. He could answer that even on our budget we can afford new shoes. Doesn't he think of that, or is it just that he doesn't want to go on with a painful conversation? Like all Chinese of his generation he's afraid of violence, irritation, signs of vulgarity. . . . He takes his hands out of his sleeves, gestures with open arms, and rises. And that's it."

Garine lays the last sheet on the table, crosses his hands over it, and repeats, "That's it."

"Meaning?"

"I think my question's answered. The only thing to do now is wait until he's out of our hair before we talk about the decree again. Happily he's doing all he can to help us."

"How?"

"Demanding the terrorists' arrest. (He can demand it all he wants, by the way; if he gets an indictment, the police just won't find them, that's all.) Hong's hated him for a long time now."

Barging into Garine's room as I usually do when he's late, I hear shrieks: two Chinese girls on the bed, naked (long glossy stretches of hairless body), startled by my entrance, jump up shrilling and hide behind a folding screen. Garine is buttoning his officer's tunic; he calls the boy and instructs him to pay the women when they're dressed and send them on their way.

"After you've been here a while," he tells me on the staircase, "Chinese women get on your nerves. You'll see. The best thing is to sleep with them and forget about it so you can keep your mind on serious things."

"And after two at a time, you can be twice as serious?"

"If you feel like it, have them—or her, if you insist— brought to your room. We have plenty of spies in the houses along the river, but I'm leery of that kind of thing."

"Whites use those houses?"

"You bet. Chinese women have talent."

But Nikolaieff is waiting for us at the bottom of the stairs; when he sees Garine he calls, "Yah, they're still at it! Listen to this!" He pulls a sheet of paper from his pocket, and as we walk to Propaganda (the morning's not too hot yet) he reads, in a fat man's slow voice: " 'Foreign missionary men and women have fled before a peaceable Chinese throng. Why, if they were not guilty? And countless children's bones have been dug up in the mission garden. Now that it is clearly established that these creatures lacking all human decency ferociously massacre innocent Chinese babies in their orgies . . .' "

"That's from Hong, right?" Garine asks.

"Dictated, as usual, because he doesn't know how to write characters. It's his third broadside."

[104]

"Yes. I've already told him to cut it out. He's beginning to bother me, Hong is."

"I think he plans to keep it up. The only time he's happy working at Propaganda is when he's composing anti-Christian tracts. He says they make his people happy. It may be."

"That's not the point. Send him to me when he comes in."

"He asked to see you this morning. I think he's waiting."

"Mm. Whatever you do, don't ask him what he plans to do about Ch'eng-tai. Snoop around somewhere else."

"Right. Garine?"

"What?"

"Did you know the banker Hsia Ch'ou is dead?"

"Knife?"

"A bullet in the head after we crossed the bridges."

"Hong, you think?"

"I don't think, I know."

"You'd told him to lay off?"

"Gave him the word from you and Borodin. (By the way, Borodin's better. He'll be coming in soon, probably.) Hong does whatever he wants these days."

"He knew that Hsia Ch'ou was a heavy contributor?"

"Sure he knew it. But a lot it meant to him! Hsia Ch'ou was too rich. No robbery. As usual."

Garine nods for answer. We've arrived.

I go with Nikolaieff, pick up the file of latest reports from Hong Kong in his office, and go back downstairs. When I walk into Garine's office I bump into Hong, who's taking his leave. He talks with a thick accent in a low voice rich in barely suppressed rage: "You must pass judgment on what I write. Fair enough. But not on my feelings. To my mind torture is justified here. Because a poor man's life is one long torture. And people who teach poor men to put up with it ought to be punished, Christian priests or other people. They don't know. They don't know. You'd have to—I believe this—*force* them to understand." (He underlines the word with a jab, as if he were socking somebody.) "Not let soldiers loose on them, no, but lepers. A man's arm turns to mud, and oozes. If that man comes and talks resignation to me, well and good. But this other man here, this other man's saying something else again."

And he smiles as he leaves, a smile that exposes big teeth and suddenly adds an almost childlike expression to his face full of hate.

Worried, Garine broods. When he raises his head our eyes meet. "I've had the bishop warned," he says, "of the danger his missionaries are running. Their exodus is necessary now, but not their slaughter."

"And?"

" 'Suitable precautions will be taken,' he had me informed. 'After that, God will grant us or refuse us martyrdom. His will be done.' A few missionaries have left."

While he talks he scans his desk top, and focuses on one of the white memos scattered on his blotter: "Aha! Ch'eng-tai has left the photographer's and moved into a villa placed at his disposal by a friend who's out of town. And the wise old fox arranged a military guard for himself last night. Ah, what an improvement it would be to replace the Committee of Seven by a council of reliable dictators, to establish a Cheka and not have to count on people like Hong! There's still a lot to be done! What now? Yes, come in!"

The orderly brings in a silken scroll sent from Shanghai, gift of a shop steward, the calligraphy in India ink stating congratulations. At the bottom a kind of postscript is added in a paler and dirtier ink:

We [four names follow] have signed this in blood, each slashing a finger, in testimony of our admiration for our Cantonese compatriots who dare to battle in so admirable a manner against imperialist England. We therefore express our respect and are confident that the battle will be maintained until final victory. Subsequently signed by: [an endless list of collective signatures (one for each local) follows].

"*Until final victory*," Garine repeats. "The decree, the decree, the decree! It means everything. If we can't embargo Hong Kong ships from Canton, then we're just breaking our backs for nothing. The decree *has* to pass. It *has* to. Otherwise what the hell are we doing here?"

He picks up a bundle of dispatches from Hong Kong. They're all pleas for money.

"In the meantime there's only one thing to do," he goes on, "back off on the general strike. The whole of Asia's finally watching the battle we mounted: it'll be enough if the world sees Hong Kong paralyzed. A strike of seamen, longshoremen, and coolies, monitored by the whole union council—that ought to do it. Hong Kong without hands is as good as Hong Kong empty, and we need the money we'd save, we need all the Comintern's money we can get right here."

And he goes to work on a report: decisions involving the Comintern are taken by Borodin. His pouches and wrinkles are sharp in the strong light. China's most ancient authority shows its face again: the hospitals of Hong Kong, abandoned by their nurses and orderlies, are full of the sick; and on this paper yellowed by the light still another sick man writes to still another sick man. . . .

2 P.M.

Hong's new attitude worries Garine. Garine counts on him to free us from Ch'eng-tai; but even though informers' reports tell us that Hong won't wait to be indicted before acting—and that he wants to act fast, knowing that the police aren't after him yet—they still tell us nothing about how the terrorist plans to strike. For some time now an unusual personality has been working to Hong's surface, Garine tells me; and beneath the veneer of culture, contrived of meditations on a few virulent ideas plucked at random from books and conversations, the illiterate Chinese in him, the Chinese who cannot read characters, is rising and beginning to dominate the other, who reads French and English books. And this new personality is wholly ruled by the violence of his nature and of youth, and by the only way of life he truly knows: poverty. As an adolescent he lived among men whose universe was poverty, in the lower depths of huge Chinese cities crowded with the sick, the old, the crippled in body, mind, spirit, crowded with those who die of hunger and those many more condemned to a permanently brutish and feeble existence by a diet not fit for rats.

For people like that, whose sole hope is to survive one day more, misery is almost so pervasive that it doesn't even leave room for hate. Feelings, heart, dignity have all collapsed inward, and brief flashes of rancor and despair barely flicker here and there, like the rare wide-eyed man leaning on a staff donated by missionaries and so rising above the mass of tattered humanity ground into the dust.

But for others, those whom events make soldiers or bandits, who can still react, who invent complicated swindles for a pinch of tobacco, hate still exists, persistent and comradely. They live with it, waiting for the day when beleaguered troops are ready to call on looters and arsonists for help. Hong has liberated himself from poverty but he hasn't forgotten its lesson, or the image of the world it creates, ferocious and permeated by impotent hatred. "There are only two races of man," he says. "The poor and the others." His disgust with the rich and powerful,

formed in his childhood, is so intense that he desires neither
wealth nor power. Little by little, as he emerged from the
beggars' underworld, he discovered that what he hated
wasn't the happiness of the rich, but their good opinion
of themselves. "A poor man," he also said, "cannot know
self-respect." He might have accepted all that if he'd believed, with his ancestors, that his existence wasn't limited to this one lifetime. But bound to the present by his
overwhelming discovery of death, he now accepts nothing,
seeks nothing, discusses nothing: he hates.

In poverty he sees a sort of sickly demon, continually
confirming men's baseness, cowardice, weaknesses, their
aptitude for degradation. Unquestionably he hates most
the man who respects himself, is sure of himself; he couldn't
be more of a rebel against his own kind. His disgust with
respectability, a Chinese virtue par excellence, led him
into the ranks of the revolutionaries. Like all men driven
by passion, he expresses himself forcefully, which gives
him authority; and that authority is augmented by his
extreme hatred of idealists—of Ch'eng-tai in particular—
which some mistakenly lay to political reasons. He hates
idealists because they claim to "bring order to the world."
And he doesn't want order brought to the world. He
doesn't want to give up present hate for uncertain future
good. He storms against those who forget that life is
unique and who urge men to sacrifice themselves for
their children. He, Hong, is not one of those who have
children, or sacrifice themselves, or lay down truths for
others. Let Ch'eng-tai look for food in the sewers like
other men, he says, and then see how he likes hearing a
venerable old man prate upon justice! All he allows himself to see in the tormented old leader is a man who
claims, in the name of justice, the right to frustrate his,
Hong's, revenge. And thinking back to Rebecci's pathetic
confidences, he concludes that too many men have let

themselves be distracted from their true and only calling by the shadow of some ideal. He doesn't intend to end his life renting out mechanical birds, nor allow old age to creep up on him. When he heard this poem by a North Chinese:

> *I fight alone and win or lose,*
> *and no man other sets me free.*
> *I want no Jesus Christ to think*
> *that he can ever die for me*

he learned it by heart on the spot. Rebecci's influence, and then Garine's, only sharpened his need of an angry realism utterly in the service of hate. He thinks of his life as a tubercular, still strong but hopeless, might; and hate imposes a savage, brutal order on the extreme confusion of his feelings, and becomes a kind of duty.

Only action in the service of hate is free of lies, cowardice, and weakness; only such action can counter words. His need for that action made him our ally, but he's found that the International acts too slowly, and is home to too many kinds of men; twice this week he's assassinated men who were under the Comintern's protection. "Every murder boosts his self-confidence," Garine says, "and he's learning what he really is, down deep: an anarchist. Pretty soon he'll break with us. I hope not too soon!" And after a brief silence: "There are few of my enemies I understand better."

THE NEXT DAY

When I come into Garine's office, Klein and Borodin are talking, seated face to face near the door. They're keeping one eye on Hong, who's standing in the middle of the room with his hands in his pockets and talking to Garine. Borodin got out of bed this morning: yellowed, wasted, he seems Chinese today. Something in the air, in their attitudes, speaks hostility, almost wrangling. Hong talks in staccato bursts, in his thick accent, without gestures. Watching the fierce motion of his jaws (he talks as if he were biting), I suddenly remember the phrase Gérard quoted: "When I have been sentenced to capital punishment . . ."

"In France," he's saying, "they didn't dare cut off the king's head, did they? But in the end they did. And France did not die. You have to begin by cutting off the king's head, always."

"Not when he's paying."

"When he's paying. And when he isn't paying. And what does it matter to me if he pays or not?"

"It matters to us. Listen to me, Hong: a terrorist strike adapts itself to the police confronting it."

"What?"

Garine repeats the sentence. Hong seems to have understood, but he's still motionless, staring down at the tiles.

"Everything at the right time," Garine says. "The revolution's not so simple."

"Oh, the revolution . . .!"

"The revolution," Borodin says sharply, turning, "is paying the army!"

"But that's not at all interesting. Choose between them? Why? Because you're no longer on the side of justice? I leave such considerations to the respectable Ch'eng-tai. His age is his excuse. He is a pernicious old man and such niceties suit him. I am not interested in politics."

"That's right," Garine says, "make speeches! Do you know what the directors of the biggest firms in Hong Kong are doing right now, at this moment? They're lined up to ask the governor for subsidies, and the banks are refusing to put up the money. On the docks the 'nice people' are trying to do longshoreman's work, and doing it about as well as so many geese. We're ruining Hong

Kong, we're turning one of the Crown's richest colonies into a muddy little port—not to mention the example we're setting. And what are you doing?"

At first Hong is silent, but I can tell by the way he looks at Garine that he's about to speak. Finally he makes up his mind: "All social order is a lot of shit. A man's one life. Not to throw it away. That's all."

But he's only warming up.

Borodin says, "And?"

"What am I doing, you ask?" He's turned to look at Borodin this time. "What you don't dare do. To work poor men to death, that's shameful. To have poor buggers go kill the party's enemies, that's all right. But to be very careful not to dirty your own hands with either kind of thing, that's all right too, hah?"

"Maybe I'm afraid?" Borodin answers, his anger rising.

"Of being killed, no." And nodding grandly, "Of the rest, yes."

"Each of us plays his part."

"Aha! Well, this is mine, right?" Hong, too, is angered, and his accent is thicker with every sentence. "Do you think I never loathe it? It's *because* it's painful that I don't always make somebody else do it, you understand? Sure, you're looking at Monsieur Klein. He knocked off a great nobleman, I know. I asked him." Letting the sentence trail off, he looks from Borodin to Klein and laughs nervously. "All the bourgeois aren't factory executives," he murmurs. Suddenly he shrugs, violently, and goes out almost running, slamming the door behind him.

Silence.

Garine says, "That didn't do much good."

"What do you think he'll do?" Klein asks.

"About Ch'eng-tai? Ch'eng-tai's practically asked for his head." And after a moment's thought: "He understood me when I told him terrorists have to reckon with the police they face. So he'll try to finish off Ch'eng-tai as soon as possible. Most likely. But beginning now we're all targets. . . . Step right up, gents; who's first?"

Chewing on his mustache, Borodin buckles his Sam Browne belt—it gives him trouble—and gets up and leaves. We follow him out. Flattened against the light bulb, a huge butterfly throws a broad black shadow on the wall.

9 P.M.

Probably Myroff's advice worried Garine; for the first time he talks about his sickness unasked. "Disease, old buddy, disease, well, you can't know what it's like when you're not sick. You think it's something to fight off, something outside you. Nope. Disease is your*self*. Anyway, as soon as the Hong Kong problem's solved . . ."

After dinner, a telegram: Ch'en Chiung-ming's army has left Wai-ch'ao and is marching on Canton.

When I wake up I hear that Garine was taken to the hospital last night after an attack of fever. I'll be able to see him after six this evening.

Hong and the anarchists announce meetings for this afternoon, in the main union halls. Hong himself will make a speech to "The Junk," the strongest coolie organization in the port of Canton, and then to several lesser groups. To answer him Borodin has chosen Mao Ling-wu, one of the Kuomintang's best orators.

Tomorrow our agents will announce the end of the general strike in Hong Kong and at the same time, to keep the pressure on, double agents will tell the police that the Chinese are infuriated at the strike's failure and preparing an armed uprising. The last few days British firms have been trying to set up a transshipping service in

Swatow, so merchandise offloaded there can be delivered to the interior. Yesterday the Swatow unions called a coolies' strike by our order; this morning the confiscation of British goods was ordered. Finally, an extraordinary court has just adjourned: all businessmen who accepted delivery of British merchandise will be arrested and punished by a fine amounting to two-thirds of their assets. Anyone failing to pay within ten days will be executed.

5 P.M.

I've been kept very late, and the meeting of "The Junk" must have started.

We—Nikolaieff's Yunnanese assistant and I—stop in front of a factory of some sort, enter a garage and pass through it, marching down a lane between lines of Fords, and then cross a courtyard. Again, a plain roof, a vast white wall splotched green by the rains as if buckets of acid had been sloshed on it, and a door. At the door, sitting on a crate, a sentry in rope-soled sandals is showing his automatic to a bunch of kids, the tinier ones naked. My companion presents a card; to read it, the sentry rises and gently shoos the pigtailed children. We go on in. A muffled roar rises in a thick, bluish fog, and now and then a word or sentence detaches itself. At first all I can see is two broad sunbeams swarming with specks of dust, shining through the windows, and plunging into the shadowy hall like slanting golden rails. Light, dust, smoke: a swirling, rich stuff with floral patterns sketched in by tobacco. Slowly the chaotic uproar jells around the speaker's panting voice—he's in shadow—and becomes the rhythmic shout "Yes! Yes!" or "No! No!" torn from the crowd by every sentence and punctuating the speech like hoarse strokes of a gong; a litany.

Slowly my eyes adapt to the gloom. No decorations in

the hall. Three platforms: one for the officers, the president and two advisers, beneath a huge hanging covered with characters (Sun Yat-sen's last testament, maybe? I can't read it, it's too far off); another that the speaker stands on, and we can't see him any better than we hear him; and a third, where an old Chinese with a fine, arched nose and crew-cut gray hair stands in plain sight, in a kind of pulpit. He's leaning forward propped on his elbows, and waiting.

I begin to see the crowd more clearly; they hardly move, hardly gesture. There are four or five hundred men in this small hall. Near the officers, a few students with their hair cut short. The big overhead fans whack heavily at the thick air. Packed in, the audience—soldiers, students, small shopkeepers, coolies—shout their approval with a quick jutting motion of the chin like a barking dog, not stirring otherwise. No folded arms, no elbows on knees, no chins in hands: rigid, upright, cadaverish bodies, impassioned faces, jutting jaws, and always staccato, the barking chorus of approval.

And now I begin to hear clearly enough to understand. It's Hong's voice, not hesitant as when he speaks French, but strong and quick. He's near the end of his speech:

"They say they've brought us freedom! For five years we've been smashing the British Empire like an egg, while they still crawl on their bellies under the lash of their military mandarins!

"They send their paid agents—their 'boys'!—to tell us that they're the ones who taught us revolution!

"Did we need them?

"Did the leaders of the T'ai P'ing rebellion have Russian advisers?

"Or the Boxers?"

His fiery, passionate street Chinese is punctuated by

guttural cries: "No! No!" Hong raised his voice a notch with each sentence. Now he shouts: "When our oppressors were about to butcher the workers of Canton, was it the Russians who shook up the cans of gasoline? And who threw those brazen pigs, those merchant volunteers, into the river?"

"No, no! Yes, yes! No, no!"

Motionless, still propped on his elbows, Mao Ling-wu remains silent. Obviously the whole audience is with the speaker, and it would be no use to tell these men that they didn't beat the merchant volunteers alone.

Hong's got what he wanted; he must have been talking for quite a while. He leaves the platform—he has commitments to other rallies—and walks out quickly amid an admiring uproar that drowns out Mao Ling-wu, who's begun to speak. Can't hear a word. The rally was well prepared; it seems to me that the protests and catcalls come from seven or eight Chinese, always the same ones, scattered around the hall. Unquestionably the crowd would like to listen, in spite of its hostility: Mao is a famous old orator. But he doesn't raise his voice. He goes on talking amid the clamor, taking a careful look at the various focuses of opposition. Ah. He's noticed how few hecklers have been carrying the audience along. Then in a strong, suddenly clear voice, and with a sweep of his arm to include them all: "Look at these men who insult me and interrupt me, fearing my words!"

A stir, an eddy. He's won: everybody's turned toward one or another of the anarchists. Mao's opposition isn't the whole hall now; only his isolated enemies.

"Those who live off English money while our strikers die of hunger are worse than . . ."

Impossible to hear the end. Mao is leaning forward, his mouth wide open. On every note of the Chinese scale, screeching insults rise throughout the hall, the shouts of a mob. A few ring out clearly: "Dog! Sellout! Traitor! Traitor! Coolie!"

Mao may be talking; I don't hear him. Meanwhile the uproar subsides. A few isolated insults, like the last applause in a theater . . . Then he recaptures his audience by lifting both hands and raising his voice sharply: "Coolie? Yes. Coolie! I have always moved among the poor. But not to shout their name as you do between the names of thieves and traitors! When I was hardly more than a child—"

(Scuffling between the anarchists and the listeners; but they're listening.)

"—I swore to bind my life to theirs, and no one will release me from that vow, for all those to whom I swore it are dead." And, arms flung forward, hands open: "You the homeless, you the riceless, all of you! You the nameless, you who bear the mark, wood-porters and boat-pullers with welted shoulders, dockers with welted backs —hear, hear those whose glory is bought with your blood! Hear how they sneer, *Coolies!*, these fine gentlemen, in the same tone I used for *Dogs!*, speaking of them just now!"

"Yes, yes!" Rhythmic acclamation again. "Yes, yes!"

"Death to those who insult the people!" Who called out? No one knows. The voice was feeble, halting. But immediately a hundred voices shout, "Deaaaaath!" It's a roll of thunder, a confused growl that grows to a roar. We can hardly make out the word; the tone is enough.

Some anarchists try to climb to the platform, but Mao didn't show up alone; now his men block the way, with the crowd's help. One anarchist sitting on another's shoulders tries to make himself heard. They charge him, fling him to the floor, and beat him. A brawl. We take off. At the door I turn: in the even thicker smoke the light clothes, the white robes, the worn blue and brown

[117]

dockworkers' outfits are jumbled together, a restless, confused mob bristling with upraised fists and chalk-white caps. . . .

In the street I notice Mao leaving. I try to catch up with him but fail. Possibly he'd rather not be seen with a white man today.

I head for the hospital alone and on foot. The way Mao got out of a bad spot was a credit to his talent, but if some fool hadn't yelled "Coolie!" what would have happened? A victory owed to a silly accident is an empty victory. Besides, Mao was defending only himself. When my Yunnanese companion left me he said, "And don't forget, Monsieur, if Hong had still been there Mao might not have won so easily."

Won?

I reach the hospital in full darkness. At each corner of the pavilion, under the palms, soldiers stand, pistols at the ready. I go on in. The corridors are deserted at this time of evening. Only a sleeping orderly, lying on a settee of carved wood near the door, wakes when he hears the click of my heels on the tiles, and shows me to Garine's room.

Linoleum, whitewashed walls, a sizable fan, the smell of medication, mainly ether. The mosquito net is half rolled up; Garine seems to be sleeping in a four-poster with tulle curtains. I sit down at his bedside. The wicker arms slip beneath my moist hands. My weary body relaxes; outside, the eternal mosquitoes whine. A palm leaf hangs below the eaves, a rigid, metallic pattern against the soft and formless night. On the warm air rise the mingled odors of sickly-sweet garden flowers and decomposition, tainted at times by another: stagnant water, tar, and iron. Somewhere in the distance, the clack of mah-jongg tiles, shouts in Chinese, horns, firecrackers; when the river wind floats to us, swampy, and we're quiet, we hear a single-stringed violin: some street theater or some craftsman playing, half asleep in his shuttered booth. A smoky reddish light glows beyond the trees, as if some great fair were coming to an end: the city.

With his eyes half shut and his hair straggling down on his drawn face, Garine asks as soon as he sees me, "Well?"

"Nothing important." I give him some news and then shut up. In the hall and in the room bulbs glow, swarming with insects, as if they'd glow forever. The orderly's footfalls recede. "Do you want me to leave you alone?"

"No, not at all. I don't want to be alone. I don't like thinking about myself, and when I'm sick I do it all the time." The weariness of his voice—ordinarily so sharp but trembling a little tonight, as if his mind had lost control of his speech—goes well with the dim bulbs, the silence, the smell of sweaty bodies sometimes overwhelming the smell of ether or the smell of the garden, where soldiers patrol; goes well with this whole hospital where only the swarming masses of insects, buzzing around the bulbs, seem alive. . . .

"Funny. After my trial I really felt—strongly—that all life was useless, that humanity was a slave to absurd impulses. Now I feel it again. Damn foolishness, being sick. Still, I get the feeling that I'm fighting human absurdity, doing what I do here. The absurd reasserting its rights." He twists in his bed, and the acid smell of fever rises. "Ah, that indescribable wholeness that lets us feel our lives are good for something . . . Odd how strong memory is when you're sick. All day I've been thinking about my trial. I wonder why. After the trial my feeling that any social order was absurd expanded slowly until it included everything human. That doesn't bother me,

[119]

by the way. And yet, and yet . . . Right now, at this very moment, how many men are dreaming of victories that two years ago they could never even have imagined! I created their hope. Their hope. I'm not much for fancy talk, but what the hell, man's hope is his reason to live and die. So? Well, a man shouldn't talk so much with a high fever. Foolish. To think about yourself all day! Why do I think about that trial? Why? It was so long ago! Silly. A fever. But you see things. . . ."

The orderly has just opened the door quietly. Garine turns over again; again the human smell of disease seeps through the smell of ether.

"In Kazan, on Christmas night in 1919, that crazy parade. Borodin was there, as usual. . . . What? They carry all the gods to the cathedral, huge figures like on floats at Mardi Gras, a goddess-fish in a bathing suit. . . . Two or three hundred gods . . . Luther, too. Musicians bundled in furs making a hell of a racket with all the instruments they could round up. A Yule log burning. Up on people's shoulders, the gods circle the plaza, black against the blazing log, or against the snow. . . . A victory dance! The tired bearers fling their gods on the fire. It flares, splits the heads open, lights the cathedral white against the night. . . . What? The revolution? Yes. It goes on like that for seven or eight hours. I couldn't wait for dawn! Corruption, decay . . . the things a man sees. You can't throw the revolution on the fire; whatever isn't it, is worse than it, you have to admit that even when you're fed up with it. . . . Like the self. Not with, not without. In school I learned that, in Latin. We'll sweep it all away. What? Maybe it was snowing, too. . . . What?"

He's on the verge of delirium. Excited by the sound of his own voice, he talks louder; it echoes through the hospital. The orderly whispers in my ear, "The doctor said we must not allow the Commissar of Propaganda to talk too long." And out loud, "Commissar, would you like some chloral to help you sleep?"

THE NEXT DAY

Robert Norman, the government's American adviser, left Canton last night. For several months he'd only been consulted on questions of minor importance. He may have believed that he wasn't safe now—and not without reason. To replace him Borodin has at last been officially designated adviser to the government, and overall commander of the army and the air force. So Galen, who commands the Cantonese general staff, will now be responsible to Borodin alone, which means that the armed forces are in the hands of the Comintern.

PART THREE

———

THE MAN

Dispatches from Hong Kong tell the world that the city's easing back to normal. But they add: ONLY THE DOCKERS HAVE NOT GONE BACK TO WORK. Nor will they. The harbor's still empty: more and more the city looks like that great black empty silhouette I saw pasted against the sky when I left it. Pretty soon Hong Kong will have to find some line of work that suits an isolated island. Its main source of revenue, the rice trade, is slipping away: the big producers have made deals with Manila and Saigon. In a letter we intercepted, a member of the Chamber of Commerce wrote, "If the British don't send troops, within a year Hong Kong will be the shakiest port in the Far East."

Volunteer units patrol the city. Many businessmen's cars have been fitted out with machine guns. Last night barbed-wire barricades were set up around the telephone exchange—no defense without telephones. Other defenses are under construction around the reservoirs, the governor's mansion, and the Arsenal. And though they express confidence in the militia, the British police, caught napping, are sending message after message, envoy after envoy, to General Ch'en Chiung-ming, pressing him to march on Canton.

"You understand, my dear friend," Nikolaieff says to me in his priest's voice, "Garine would do better to leave. A lot better. Myroff talked to me about him. If he stays another two weeks, he'll stay a lot longer than he wants.

Of course, you're no sicker buried here than anywhere else."

"He says he can't leave now."

"I know. Well, sick people are nothing unusual around here. The way we live, we're never quite safe from the tropics." He points to his big belly, with a grin. "I prefer this problem. And when what really matters to him isn't at stake, Garine can be wishy-washy. Like everybody."

"And you don't think his life matters to him?"

"Not much, not much."

A report from one of Ch'eng-tai's boys—our spy—is just in.

Ch'eng-tai knows that the terrorists want to assassinate him. He's been advised to flee; he's refused. But the spy heard him say to a friend, "If my life isn't enough to stop them, perhaps my death will be." And he wasn't talking about murder, but suicide. If Ch'eng-tai killed himself for a cause, in the Asian tradition, he'd reinforce that cause dangerously. "He's capable of it," Nikolaieff says. And the police are jittery.

Garine has just left the hospital. Myroff or the Chinese doctor will come over every morning to give him a shot.

THE NEXT DAY

It's not just Ch'eng-tai who worries Nikolaieff; yesterday Ch'en Chiung-ming took Ch'ao-ch'ao, whipped a detachment of Cantonese troops, and headed for Canton. The Cantonese troops were former mercenaries for Sun Yat-sen, and Borodin considers them worthless, useless in combat unless led and stiffened by the cadets and the red army. But the cadets, under Chiang Kai-shek's orders, are staying in Whampoa; the red army, under Galen's orders, is not leaving its garrisons. Only Propaganda agents, who can pave the way for victory but not win it, will leave the city tomorrow. "Let the Committee of Seven decide," Garine says. "Now it's either the red army *and the decree*, or Ch'en Chiung-ming. And Ch'en Chiung-ming means the firing squad. It's up to them!"

THAT NIGHT

Eleven o'clock at Garine's. Klein and I are sitting near the window waiting for him. On a small table next to Klein, a bottle of rice wine and a glass. A police orderly brought the blue poster lying there, carelessly folded, on the table the boys forgot to clear. They're pasting up the same poster all over the city.

It's the final paragraph of Ch'eng-tai's last testament:

I, Ch'eng-tai, have taken my own life of my own free will in order to impart this to all my fellow countrymen: PEACE, our greatest treasure, must not be squandered along the false trails down which foreign advisers are preparing to lead the Chinese people....

These posters alone can stop us colder than all Ch'eng-tai's preaching; and who's pasting them up at this time of night?

Did he kill himself? Was he murdered?

Garine's gone to the police and to Borodin's. First he had them try to verify Ch'eng-tai's death, but he left without waiting for the answer, and doubtless found a copy of it at police headquarters. It's just been delivered to us: Ch'eng-tai is dead of a knife wound in the chest. Edgy, swatting our legs at every least mosquito bite, we wait. I hear Klein's voice, faint and remote, as if he too were feverish: "I knew him. I tell you it just isn't possible."

I said that the suicide seemed likely to me, and Klein, protesting, is trying to control an inexplicable vehemence. I've always found something odd about this man, whose appearance—he looks like an army boxing coach—masks considerable culture. Garine is his very close friend, and told me, when I asked, what Gérard had already told me: "It's a little like the Legion here, and all I know about his past is what everybody knows." Like a statue tonight, with his thick arms propped on the chair's, he has great trouble saying what he means, and not because he's speaking French. His eyes shut, he hunches at each sentence, as if he were fighting his own words. He's drunk in a sharp, alert way—muscles and thoughts at the stretch—and it gives his voice a tough, fervent tone. "Not possible."

Lulled by the singsong rhythm of the droning fan, I stare at him.

"You just can't know! It's . . . I can't express it. You have to know people who've tried. It takes forever. First you say, in an hour, a half-hour, peace and quiet. Then you think, well, now, this is it. And suddenly you're in a daze, staring foolishly at the light: you smile like an imbecile and you know you're not going to think about *that* anymore. At all. But still . . . And then it all sweeps back over you. And at that point the idea's stronger than you are. Not the act itself; just the idea. You say to yourself, Ach, why all this fuss?"

I ask him casually, "Do you think you come to love life more?"

"Life, death—by that time you don't know what they are! Only: *I must do this thing.* I had my elbows in tight against my ribs and both hands on the hilt of the knife. All I had to do was ram it home. No. You can't imagine what it's like: I could have just shrugged and done it. Silly, it was, foolish! I'd even forgotten my reasons. I had to do it because I had to do it, that was all. And then I was astounded. Ashamed, mainly ashamed. I was so disgusted I figured I ought to throw myself into the canal. Stupid, wasn't it? Yes. Stupid. Lasted quite a while. Daylight pulled me out of it. You can't kill yourself in daylight. I mean, not if you're thinking about it. In a split-second, just like that, without giving it much thought, maybe you can. But not . . .

"It took me a while to find my bearings."

He laughs a laugh so artificial that I step to the window, as if to see whether Garine's back yet. Over the drone of the fan I hear Klein's nails tapping on the wicker. He's talking to himself. Heavily, trying to dispel his worries by insisting, by showing me that he views the whole matter sanely, he goes on: "It's not easy. For people who do it because they're up to here with everything, there are ways to get to the point almost without realizing it. . . . But Ch'eng-tai would kill himself for something he believes in, you understand? Something he believes in more than all the rest. More. So if he does it, it's the noblest act of his life. That's why he couldn't have done it that way. Impossible. Wouldn't have been worth it."

"The example would be the same."

"You just don't understand. An example, you say. How hard it is! It's something like the Japanese, you know? Ch'eng-tai isn't doing it to be worthy of himself. Or to live . . . *muthig* . . . what is that, in French? Heroically, yes. For Ch'eng, it's to be worthy of what—of his mission. So he couldn't—you follow?—kill himself by surprise! And yet—"

He falls silent abruptly, listening. A car stops, a hum of voices: "I'll expect you at six." The car drives off.

Garine.

"Klein, Borodin's waiting for you." He turns to me: "Let's go upstairs." And as soon as we're there: "What was he telling you?"

"That Ch'eng couldn't have killed himself."

"I know. He always claimed Ch'eng could never do that to us. Remains to be seen."

"What do you think?"

"Nothing very definite yet."

"And him?"

"Who, him? Borodin? No. You're wrong to smile. We had nothing to do with it. That much I know. Not even indirectly, not even accidentally. He was as shocked as I was."

"Come on now. And all the hints we gave Hong?"

"Ah! That's something else again. According to the first reports, we can't be sure that Hong had anything to do with it either. The guard platoon was never off sentry duty, and no one went in. But that doesn't matter much now. We have more important things to do. First, the posters. Take this down and translate it: 'Let us never forget that a man respected by all China, Ch'eng-tai, was assassinated yesterday by the cowardly agents of our enemies.' And for another poster to be stuck up *right beside it*: 'All shame to England, all shame to the assassins of Shanghai and Canton!' And in the corner of the second one, in small characters, '20 May–25 June' (the Shanghai and Shameen incidents).

"Good. They'll understand that. Now, the communiqué to all branches: Ch'eng-tai did not commit suicide, he was assassinated by British agents. Nothing will prevent us from meting out swift justice. Gaudy but neat."

"You're throwing the terrorists to the dogs?"

"Hong Kong comes first. This may squeeze the decree out of them." He sits at his desk. While I translate he draws crazy birds on his blotter, stands up, paces, comes back to the desk, does a little more drawing, drops his pencil again, inspects his revolver carefully, and finally sits meditating with his chin in his hands. I hand him the two translations.

"Absolutely sure these are accurate?"

"Absolutely sure. Now, would you mind telling me what it's all for?"

"That's obvious."

"Not very."

"We paste them up on the walls, all right?"

Bewildered, I squint at him. "But before your poster's even printed, everybody'll have read the other one, no?"

"No."

"You going to have them torn down? That's hard work and it takes time."

"No! I'm having them covered over. We're assigning our own troops to odd jobs; they won't be back in town before noon. At five o'clock our irregulars will be in the streets firing rifles. The police have been warned. The middle class won't stick its nose outside for hours. The others are illiterate. Anyway almost all the other posters will be covered within three hours. By eight o'clock tomorrow—or today; it's one in the morning—there'll be five thousand of ours on the walls. We're printing up a hundred thousand as fliers. The twenty or even fifty posters we forget to cover won't matter a damn against all that—even less, because they won't be read before ours."

"And if they use this death as pretext for a coup?"

"Can't be helped. But it's too soon. They have hardly any troops and they wouldn't dare all by themselves. And even if the public doesn't believe us absolutely, they'll hesitate. You can't make a popular uprising with hesitaters. No. It'll be all right."

"If he didn't kill himself——"

"If he *had* killed himself we'd have worse problems."

"—then the ones who gain by that blue poster 'suicided' him?"

"Whoever printed up that blue poster is in the same position as us. They got their information earlier, that's all. And they made use of it as fast as they could. And now we're printing posters, too. We'll know where we stand soon enough. But first things first. This killing could have been part of a deal."

We're almost running down the stairs.

"And Borodin?"

"I looked in on him for a few seconds. He's sick. Every man in his turn. I wonder if anyone's tried to poison him. His boys are reliable, and also—"

He stops short. Rushing down the stairs behind me, he's missed a step and just managed to grab the railing. He pauses a few seconds, catches his breath, smooths his hair back, and hurries on down, still talking: "—and also carefully watched."

The car.

"To the printer's."

We lay our pistols on the seat, handy. The city seems quite calm. Riding along we hardly notice the lights we pass, flickering on us like stripes, or the occasional faint glow through cracks in the badly joined planks that shutter the small shops at night. No moon, no houses outlined against the sky. What life there is clings to the earth; lanterns, street vendors, cheap cook shops, lamp flames erect in the hot airless night, quick shadows, motionless figures, phonographs, phonographs. . . . But in the distance, rifle fire.

Here's the printer's. Our printer. A long shed. Inside, the light dazzles; we have to shut our eyes. All the workers here are party members, carefully screened; tonight there's a military guard at each door anyway. The soldiers have been expecting us. A very young lieutenant, a cadet, reports to take Garine's orders. "Nobody comes in or goes out." The work in progress is interrupted. I hand the two translations to the master printer—a Chinese—who slices them carefully into vertical strips and gives one line to each compositor.

"Correct the proofs," Garine tells me, "and bring me the first sheet printed. I'll be at police headquarters. If not, wait for me there. I'll have a car sent for you."

Quickly the two texts are set up. The master printer pastes the lines side by side and passes me the proofs; no single worker knows what's on the poster he helped to print.

Two presses have stopped while the pressmen wait for the forms we're about to give them. A few mistakes. A couple of minutes more for the corrections. And the forms are on the presses, wedged in by hand and even bare feet.

I take the first sheet printed and leave.

A car's waiting, and we race to police headquarters. In the distance, a few shots. At the door a cadet greets me, then leads me to the office where Garine is waiting, through empty corridors (lit by occasional bulbs, each haloed) where our footsteps echo loud and clear in the silence of the night. I've begun to feel a general weariness mingled with excitement, and my mouth tastes of sleepless nights: fever and alcohol.

A large office, brightly lit. Garine's pacing, his face drawn and his hands in his pockets. Nikolaieff's lying on a Chinese wardroom bed of carved wood against one wall.

"Well?"

I hand him the poster. "Careful. The ink's not dry. I got it all over my hands."

He shrugs, spreads the poster, looks at it, and compresses his lips as if nibbling at them. (He's peeved not to know Cantonese or the written characters, or rather to know a little of both and very badly; and he has no time these days to learn.) "You sure it's right?"

"Don't worry about it. Listen, do you know there's fighting in the streets?"

"Fighting?"

"I can't be sure. But I heard shots on the way."

"Many shots?"

"No. Few and far between."

"That's all right, then. It's our own men picking off theirs, the ones pasting up the blue posters." He turns back to Nikolaieff, who's propped up on an elbow. "Go on. Can you think of anybody on the other side who's not very brave and may know something?"

"By 'somebody not very brave' you mean . . . ?"

"Yes."

"I don't believe any man's very brave under those circumstances."

"Yes. Some are." Garine's arms are folded, his eyes shut; Nikolaieff looks at him strangely, almost with hate. "Hong wouldn't talk."

"We could try. . . ."

"No use."

"You think a lot of your old buddies. All right, then. If you want . . ."

Garine shrugs. "Yes or no?"

The other is silent. We wait. "Ling, maybe."

"No. Come on, now. No 'maybe.' "

"But you're the one who makes me say 'maybe.' As far as I'm concerned there's no doubt. When you've seen men prowling the corpses at night after a massacre, looking for their relatives, their wives, or when you've seen the Chinese interrogate prisoners, you know all you need to know about that."

"Ling's a union boss?"

"The harbor coolies' union."

"Do you think he knows what happened?"

"We'll find out. In my opinion, yes."

"Good. Do it."

Nikolaieff stretches forward to lean on the arm of a chair, and rises with an effort. "I think we can have him by tomorrow." And half smiling, with an odd look of ironic deference: "And what shall we do with him?"

Garine answers with an impatient gesture. "It doesn't matter." A look of slight scorn crosses Nikolaieff's face. Garine broods at him, chin up like a bulldog's, and says, "Incense."*

The fat man closes his eyes in agreement, lights a cigarette, and walks out ponderously.

THE NEXT DAY

I leave my car outside the marketplace. The long buildings fringe the pellucid blue sky with streaks of plaster, rippling in the fluid light. Every stall that sells a beverage is jammed with men in brown or blue outfits like the dockers'. Just as the car stops, shouts ring out, sustained cries borne on the transparent air as on a river. And the men stream quickly out of the stalls, fumbling in their pockets to tuck away the small change of the coins they've just spent, hurrying and jostling. In single file they board the commandeered buses and trucks waiting for them at the end of the white wall. The leaders shout again: a few men are not accounted for. But here they come, running, they too shouting, or gripping tiny sausages in their teeth, or hitching up their pants. . . . And one by one the trucks shake themselves heavily into life and roar off.

* Slow strangulation; incense then revives the patient.

The Second Propaganda Company, spearheading the red army, is on the march.

Our posters are pasted on every wall. Ch'eng-tai's counterfeit testament—covered over everywhere now—printed in the hope of a popular uprising, but without preparation, came too late; there's no sign of an uprising. Was T'ang's defeat a lesson? Does fear at Ch'en Chiung-ming's approach to Canton counter any new agitations?

The cadets are circulating throughout the city.

All morning agents troop into Garine's office; after a sleepless night his face is even gaunter. Drooping over his desk, his head on his left hand, he dictates or issues orders; he's worn to a frazzle. He's had new posters printed up: THE END OF HONG KONG. They claim that the English are leaving the city in droves and the banks have announced the permanent closing of their local branches. (The posters lie. The banks, on orders from London, continue to support British enterprises as far as they can—though with bad grace.) But on the other hand, to force the Committee of Seven to stand behind him, he has our agents spread the word that Ch'ao-ch'ao has fallen and that the red army—the only army the people trust—is not yet in position.

By noontime special editions of the newspapers, plus posters and cloth sandwich boards walked all over the city, have announced that Hong Kong's merchants and manu-facturers (almost the whole European population), meeting yesterday in their biggest theater, telegraphed the King demanding the dispatch of British troops to China. That much is accurate.

Borodin's told the Committee that he doesn't object to the antiterrorist decrees Ch'eng-tai proposed; and those decrees will be in force beginning today. But our spies agree that no anarchist meetings will take place. Ling hasn't been arrested yet, and Hong has disappeared. The terrorists have decided to lie low except for "direct action" —that is, executions.

Ch'en Chiung-ming is still advancing.

In Hong Kong huge headlines announce TOTAL DEFEAT OF THE CANTONESE ARMY. In hotel lobbies and news bureaus the British wait nervously for news from the front. But in the harbor only slow junks leave wakes; the steamers lie dead in the water, like wrecks sinking slowly.

Among the Chinese in power here, tension is high. Ch'en's entry into Canton will mean torture for them, or execution on a street corner by firing squads working so fast that their officers won't even have time to list the victims' identities. The idea of death is in every conversation, in men's eyes, in the air, constant, present like light. . . .

Garine's rehearsing a speech for Ch'eng-tai's funeral tomorrow.

A distant rumble of drums and gongs, the piercing shriek of single-stringed violins and flutes, suddenly shrill then suddenly mellow; the thin, delicate (and screechy) sound of bagpipes; all amid a great uproar—clacking and muffled at once—of wooden sandals and shouted slogans fanfared by gongs.

I lean out the window. The cortege files past at the end of the street. A gaggle of children scooting along with their heads turned to look back, like so many goslings; a shapeless cloud of dust advancing; a vague crowd of white-cloaked figures with silken banners seemingly stitched among them, crimson, purple, cerise, pink, vermilion, carmine, every shade of red. The crowd lines

[137]

both sides of the street, and I can hardly see the cortege: only two tall masts supporting a white calico banner and swaying like a sailboat's masts, dipping in time to the sinister bang of the huge drums that drown out all the voices. "Death to the English!" And then only the crowds lining the street, the dust rising slowly and the music hammered out on gongs.

And now the offerings: heaps of fruit, enormous tropical still lifes, topped off by scrolls covered with characters; these too, borne by men, tremble and sway as if about to fall. Then comes the catafalque, the traditional long pagoda of red and black carved wood, on the shoulders of thirty husky men whose heads I can just glimpse. I can imagine the quick march, then the halt, then the strides in unison making the huge dark-red mass pitch and toss like a ship.

And what's this, next? It looks like a calico house. It is: a house of taut cloth on a bamboo armature, it too borne by men and moving forward in fits and starts. Quickly I step to the next room and take Garine's binoculars from his desk drawer. I come back: the house is still there. Large portraits are painted on its walls: Ch'eng-tai is pictured dead, below a British soldier bayoneting him. The painting is framed by a legend in vermilion characters: I can just see DEATH TO THE BRITISH BANDITS as the bizarre symbol disappears, cut off by a street corner as if by an onstage flat. Now all I can make out is a flock of small placards in the wake of the cloth house like birds following a ship, these too proclaiming hatred of England. Then lanterns, staves, caps brandished; then nothing. And the crowd lining the street disperses while the sound of drums and gongs recedes and the dust, still rising slowly, dissolves into the light.

A few hours later, long before Garine gets back, excerpts from his speech begin to buzz through Propaganda, from clerk to clerk and agent to agent. Obliged like Borodin to do his public speaking through a Chinese interpreter, Garine talks in short sentences and slogans. Today I hear these, at one time or another in one office or another: "Hong Kong, flaunting its ill-gotten turnkey's loot in the face of our own famine . . . Hong Kong, the prison guard . . . Not those who talk, but those who act; not those who protest, but those who drive the English out of Hong Kong like rats . . . Like the honest man severing the hand of a thief at his window with one stroke, tomorrow you will see the severed hand of British imperialism, a bankrupt Hong Hong. . . ."

A crowd of workers passes in the street, and I can read the banners they carry: LONG LIVE THE RED ARMY. They gather under the windows outside the offices where the Committee of Seven sits. Now near and now far, like a flock scattering and regrouping, shouts of "Long live the red army" fill the street, isolated, in series, or in swelling chorus. With those shouts China comes to life, China makes her presence felt, the China I'm just beginning to know, the China where the impulses of a fierce idealism are overcoming the base and selfish reflexes of oppressed masses; just as, in the smells filtering through my open windows above the seething city, the smell of pepper overcomes the smell of rot.

Outside, LONG LIVE THE RED ARMY and Ch'eng-tai enshrined by public ceremony; here on my desk, reeking up from my files, the stench of vile ambition, special favors, electoral corruption, bribes to the party, extortion, the sale of opium, the open purchase of office, undisguised blackmail—a world that lives by exploiting the Three People's Principles just as it would have by exploiting the mandarinate. An element of the Chinese bourgeoisie that the revolutionaries hate bitterly is on their side, infiltrating their revolution. "We'll have to blast through that," Garine said to me one day, "like a well-aimed kick through a dungheap."

THE NEXT DAY

No news of the terrorists: Ling, the man Nikolaieff mentioned, is still at large. Since Borodin's nomination (he's still sick, and can't leave the house) six of our men have been assassinated.

And Hong Kong's holding out. The governor's appealed to Japan and French Indochina: in a few days coolies will sail from Yokohama and Haiphong to come and replace the strikers. We have to make sure that those coolies, imported at enormous expense, arrive in a Hong Kong glutted with mountains of rice without buyers, and business houses without hope. "Canton is the key with which the British opened the door to South China," Garine said in his speech yesterday. "We have to slam that door tight and throw away the key. We must announce and enforce a ban from Cantonese waters of all ships that touch at Hong Kong." In the minds of foreigners Hong Kong, British port and Crown colony, has already become a dangerously disorganized Chinese port, and foreign ships have begun to bypass it.

Mail boats and large freighters no longer put into Hong Kong for more than a few hours; they offload in Shanghai, where the British, by lining up Chinese go-betweens, are trying to build a new organization in the Chinese part of the city to transship, for sale in the interior, merchandise ordered from England by Hong Kong firms; a new version of the attempt that failed at Swatow.

The Committee of Seven has taken new steps to bring the red army into the field and compel the arrest of terrorist leaders. The Committee's representative promises that the decree Garine demands will be signed within three days. All day a menacing (and well-organized) mob, roaring praise for the red army, has surrounded the building where the Committee sits.

THE NEXT DAY

Ling was arrested yesterday; this afternoon we'll have the information we want from him. Nervous at the advance of enemy troops, Propaganda's working furiously. The agents who infiltrate ahead of the army have been given detailed instructions; Garine has personally issued orders to their leaders. I've seen them going by in the corridor, one after another, all smiles. We've decided not to use leaflets; we have plenty of agents, enough so we can substitute word-of-mouth—the most dangerous method, the one that costs most men, but the surest. Liao Chung-k'ai, the government's commissar of finance (whom the terrorists would like to assassinate), has managed to raise large amounts of money thanks to a new system of tax collection worked out by the Comintern's experts, and once again Propaganda's well funded. In a few weeks the enemy's supply services and general administration will be thoroughly disorganized, and it's hard to make mercenaries fight without pay. Also some hundred men, whose leaders say they're absolutely reliable, are going to enlist in Ch'en Chiung-ming's army, in the full knowledge that they risk being shot by him as traitors and by our own troops as enemies. The day before yesterday three of our agents, exposed, were strangled after hours of torture.

Our Propaganda men left, marching down a corridor between two lines of half-open doors to join Ch'en's troops: chic young Chinese in belted jackets and wide trousers, who scorn native dishes and prefer to speak English, some back from American universities and some from Russian ("Lenin's bear cubs"), stood disdainful,

[1 4 1]

condescending, and watched our agents go forth to join the enemy's army.

Everything in its turn.
News from Shanghai:
The Chinese Chamber of Commerce, under instructions from the Kuomintang, has ordered the confiscation of all British goods in Chinese hands, and has forbidden the purchase of any British merchandise and the shipment of any merchandise in British bottoms, for one year beginning 30 July.
The Shanghai newspapers predict that British trade will be cut by 80 percent.
Last year that trade (Hong Kong aside) was worth twenty million pounds.
Hong Kong's last hope is Ch'en Chiung-ming's army.

Nikolaieff has received this message, in hand-printed capitals: IF LING IS NOT FREED BY TOMORROW, THE HOSTAGES WILL BE EXECUTED. Do the terrorists really hold hostages? Nikolaieff doesn't think so. But a lot of our men are out on various missions and we have no way of knowing.

6 P.M.

An orderly from the prison brings Garine some documents: Ling's interrogation.
"Did he talk?"
"One more to prove Nikolaieff right. Not many can hold out against torture."
"Did it last long?"
"Don't be silly."
"What are you going to do with him?"
"What do you want us to do with him? You can't set a terrorist leader free."
"And?"

[142]

"And the prisons are full. And anyway he'll be tried by a special court. Yes. Nikolaieff said he'd spill it all, and he did: first, where Hong is; second, that Ch'eng-tai was killed by Hong's order. The murderer was one of the boys."

"But we had spies in his house."

"One: that same boy. A double agent. He had us fooled, but not for long. We've already got him. Later on he'll do for a trial, if we need one."

"That's a little dangerous, isn't it?"

"If Nikolaieff cuts off his opium for a few days and promises he won't be executed, he'll sing like a bird."

"Are there still men who believe that kind of promise?"

"Cutting off his opium would be enough." He pauses and shrugs slowly. "It's a terribly simple matter, a man about to die." And a few moments later, in the same train of thought, "Besides, nearly all my promises have been kept."

"But how do you expect them to know——"

"What can I do about it?"

8 AUGUST

Hong was arrested last night.

In Hong Kong the British are slowly rounding up scabs to go to work in the harbor. When they have enough—Annamites and Japanese, now waiting in sheds until the governor issues instructions—they'll reorganize the labor force and the city will revive overnight. If we waver, a whole city of loaded freighters will sail for Canton, and life will flow back into the island's powerful carcass. Unless the decree we want is signed. But that decree is an acknowledgment that the unions are fighting a war; an affirmation of the intent of the Cantonese government itself—and of the Comintern's power in China.

Garine's sitting at his desk, very tired, hunched, his chin on his hands, his elbows as usual making a mess of his papers. His Sam Browne belt's flung on a chair. Hearing footsteps, he opens his eyes, runs a hand through his floppy hair, and raises his head: Hong comes in, guarded by two soldiers. He put up a fight when they arrested him: below his small, sad, glittering Asiatic eyes his face is bruised. Once in the room he halts, arms behind his back, legs apart.

Sluggish with fever, Garine looks him over and waits. Garine's played out; his body sags. His gaunt head drifts gently from side to side, as if he was about to fall asleep. Abruptly he takes a deep breath, and pulls himself together. He shrugs.

Hong has just looked up, glowering; he sees the shrug, springs free of the soldiers for a second, and drops, felled by a rifle butt. He'd seen Garine's revolver in its holster, on the chair, and was lunging for it.

He struggles to his feet.

"That's enough of that," Garine says in French. Then in Cantonese: "Take him away."

The soldiers march him off.

Silence.

"Who's going to try him, Garine?"

"When I saw him there I felt like getting up and saying, 'Now what have you been up to?' as if he were a kid playing tricks. That's why I shrugged. He thought I was insulting him. More stupidity!" Then, as if he's just heard my question, he adds quickly. "We're not trying him just yet."

Garine gives a watchmaker photos of Ch'eng-tai and Sun Yat-sen with anti-British inscriptions—models for watch cases. An orderly brings him a sealed envelope.

[144]

"Who's it from?"

"From the seamen's union hall, Commissar."

"The messenger here?"

"Yes, Commissar."

"Send him in. Go on! Quick!"

A coolie comes in, adjusting the seamen's union armband.

"You brought this?"

"Yes, Commissar."

"Where are the bodies?"

"At the union hall, Commissar."

Garine's handed me the message: the bodies of Klein and three Chinese, all murdered, have been found in one of the riverside whorehouses. *The hostages . . .*

"Where are their things?"

"I don't know, Commissar."

"You mean nobody went through their pockets?"

"No, Commissar."

Garine is up like a shot. He grabs his cap and signals me to follow. The coolie gets in beside the driver and we start up.

"He was living with a white woman, wasn't he, Garine?"

"So what!"

The bodies aren't in the office but in the meeting hall. An old Chinese keeps watch at the door, sitting on the floor. Near him is a fat dog that wants to come in; whenever the dog pads close, the Chinese, still seated, boots him away. The dog jumps a few feet in silence, then approaches again. The Chinese watches us come in. When we reach him he leans back against the wall, half closes his eyes, and shoves the door open with one hand. Not far off, the dog prowls.

We go in. A bare hall, a floor of tamped earth, heaps of dust in the corners. Even filtered by the blue skylight, the glare is dazzling, and when I glance up I see the four

[145]

bodies, *standing*. I was looking for them on the floor. They're already stiff, and somebody's set them against the wall like posts. At first I'm startled, almost stunned: there's something not fantastic, exactly, but surrealistic about these bodies, this light, this silence. Now I catch my breath, and the air I inhale is infected by an odor like no other, strong and stale at the same time, animal: the smell of dead men.

Garine calls the watchman, who stands up slowly, reluctantly, and comes in.

"Bring some sheets!"

Leaning against the door, the man looks at him stupidly. He seems not to understand.

"Bring some sheets!"

Even then he doesn't budge. Garine steps to him, fists clenched, and then halts. "Ten taels if you bring me some sheets inside half an hour. You understand?"

The Chinese bows and leaves.

The words brought a touch of humanity to the hall. But turning again, I see Klein's corpse—the tallest, it must be Klein—with a broad stain across the middle of the face: the mouth slashed from ear to ear by a razor. My muscles tighten again, this time so much that I squeeze my arms against my sides and have to lean—me too—against the wall. I avert my eyes from the open wounds, great black splotches of clotted blood, eyes turned up, all the bodies are the same. They were tortured. One of the buzzing flies lands on my forehead, and I cannot, I cannot raise my arm.

"We'll have to close his eyes, anyway," Garine says, almost whispering as he steps to Klein.

His voice snaps me out of it, and I shoo the fly with a quick, violent, clumsy gesture. Garine approaches the eyes—white eyes—with two fingers spread in a V.

His hand falls. "I think they cut off his eyelids."

Awkwardly he opens Klein's tunic, pulls out a wallet, and checks its contents. He sets aside a folded paper and looks up: the old Chinese is back, tugging at two loose awnings that balloon and drag. They were all he could find. He starts laying the corpses out side by side. But we hear footsteps, and a huddled woman comes in, tense and rigid. Garine grabs my arm roughly and pulls us back. "She too!" he murmurs. "What damn fool told her he was here?"

She doesn't look at us. She goes straight to Klein, bumps against one of the bodies, staggers. She's face to face with Klein, and stares. She doesn't stir, doesn't weep. Flies buzz around his head. The stench. In my ear, Garine's warm gasping breath.

She falls to her knees. She's not praying. She's clutching at the body, her fingers spread, clawing his flanks. It's as if she's kneeling beneath the torture all those wounds stand for, the gaping mouth slashed by a saber or a razor. I'm sure she's not praying. Her whole body trembles. And as suddenly as she fell to her knees, her arms seize the body in a convulsive embrace; she twists her head with an inexpressibly anguished roll of her breast and shoulders. With a heart-rending tenderness, yet savagely and without a sob, she rubs her face against the bloody cloth, against the very wounds.

Garine still has hold of my arm, and drags me away. At the door, the old Chinese is seated again; he doesn't even look up. But he tugs at the hem of Garine's jacket. Garine fumbles for a bill and hands it to him: "When she's gone, cover them all."

In the car he doesn't say a word. He collapses on the seat. Disease wastes him more each day. The first potholes jounce him badly and he straightens up, his head almost at the roof, his legs stiff.

Slipping out of the car in front of his house, we go up to the little room on the second floor. The blinds are down; he seems sicker and more exhausted than ever. Beneath his eyes two deep folds, parallel to the wrinkles that run from his nose to the corners of his mouth, enclose large violet pouches; and those four wrinkles, tugging at his features like death itself, seem to have begun the decomposition of his face. ("If he stays another two weeks," Myroff said, "he'll stay longer than he wants to." That was over two weeks ago.) He's silent for a while and then he says quietly, as if he were talking to himself, "Poor guy. He used to say, 'Life isn't what you think it is.' Life is never what you think it is! Never!" He sits bowed on his bunk; his hands on his knees tremble like an alcoholic's. "I loved him the way one man loves another. To see his eyelids gone . . . To think that I was about to touch his eyes . . ."

His right fist is clenched. Slumping backward, he leans against the wall, his eyes closed. His mouth and nostrils are more gaunt than ever, and a bluish shadow runs from his eyebrows halfway down his cheeks.

"Sometimes I manage to forget. . . . Sometimes. Not always. Less and less. What have I done with my own life? Good God, what *can* you do with a life? Never seeing any results! All these men I order around, men whose souls I helped create! And I don't even know what they'll be doing tomorrow. . . . Sometimes I wish I'd shaped it all like a woodcarver, so I could think, There! This is what I've done! To build, to have some time ahead of me . . . Crazy, isn't it, how we decide what we want to do?"

His fever's rising. As his excitement grows, he stresses

his words with his habitual forearm chop; but his fist is still clenched.

"What I've done, what I've done! God! I think of the emperor who had his prisoners blinded, you know, and sent them back to their own country in bunches led by one-eyed men; and the one-eyed men went blind slowly from fatigue. A pretty picture of what we're doing here, prettier than the cute little pictures Propaganda puts out. When I think that all my life I've been looking for freedom! Who's free here, in the International, the people, myself, everybody else? The people always have suicide as a last resort. That's something."

"Do you really have so little faith, Pierre?"

"I have faith in what I do. In what I do. When I . . ." He pauses. But Klein's bloody face and white eyes loom between us. "What you do, when you know that soon you'll have to quit . . ."

He thinks a while, and goes on bitterly: "I've always hated to *serve*. And who's served more than I have here, or better? For years—years!—I've wanted power, and I can't even wrap my own life in it. Klein was in Moscow when Lenin died. You know, Lenin had written an article in defense of Trotsky that was supposed to run in . . . *Pravda*, I think. His wife had delivered it. Next morning she brought him the papers. He could hardly move at all by then. 'Open it!' His article wasn't there. His voice was so hoarse that nobody understood what he said then. His gaze grew so intense that everybody followed it: he was looking at his left hand. He'd laid it flat on the sheets, palm up, like that. They saw that he wanted to pick up the paper, but couldn't."

Garine flings open his right hand, fingers stretched wide, and while he goes on talking he slowly bends his fingers again, watching them carefully.

"While his right hand lay still, his left began to clench, like a spider drawing in its legs. . . .

"He died a little later.

"Klein said, 'Like a spider. . . .' Since he told me, I've never been able to forget that hand, or those rejected articles."

"But Klein was a Trotskyite. Do you want me to fetch you some quinine?"

"My father used to say to me, 'You must never let go of the land.' He read that somewhere. He also used to say that you had to be attached to your true self: that was the Protestant in him coming out. Attached! The little ceremony of binding a living person to a corpse was called . . . republican marriage, wasn't it? I used to think it would mean more freedom. . . . He told me . . ."

"Who?"

"Klein, of course . . . that in some town or other where the Cossacks decided they had to wipe out the whole population, one fool stood there for twenty or thirty seconds with his saber raised over some kids' heads. 'Get on with it!' Klein shouted. 'I can't,' the man said. 'I feel sorry for them. I need time.'" He looks up at me, his face strangely hard. "Who else could have done what I've done here? And so what? Klein, beaten to a pulp, his mouth slit open, his lip hanging. . . . Nothing in it for me, or for any of them. Not to mention women like the one we just saw, with nothing left to do but nuzzle the wounds like a lunatic. . . . What is it? Yes, come in!"

It's a messenger from Propaganda with a note from Nikolaieff. The Cantonese troops, regrouping after their defeat at Ch'ao-ch'ao, have just been trounced again by Ch'en Chiung-ming, and the Committee's made an urgent appeal to the red army. Garine pulls a blank sheet of paper from his pocket, writes simply THE DECREE, signs it, and hands it to the messenger. "For the Committee."

[1 5 0]

"Don't you worry about riling them up?"

"We're a long way past that! I'm sick and tired of talk. I'm sick and tired of their cowardice, their cold sweat about committing themselves. They know they won't be able to revoke that decree: all the people can think about—not to mention us—is Hong Kong. And if they don't like it . . ."

"Then what?"

"Then with all the troops we have under arms, we can play T'ang's game, if we have to. I've had enough of this."

"But suppose the red army's beaten?"

"It won't be."

"If it was?"

"When you gamble, you can lose. This time we won't lose."

And as I go to find the quinine, I hear him mutter between his teeth, "There's still one thing that matters in life: not to be defeated."

THREE DAYS LATER

Garine and I are on our way home for lunch. Outside the house, four pistol shots; the soldier beside the driver moves fast. I take a quick look and then duck: they're shooting at our car. The soldier returns fire. Twenty men scatter, sleeves flapping. Two bodies on the ground. One is a bystander wounded by mistake, the other the sniper: a Luger lies close to his open hand, gleaming in the sunlight.

The soldier gets out and goes to him. "Dead," he shouts, without even bending. He calls for bearers and a stretcher to take the other Chinese—shot in the belly—to the hospital. With a jolt the car roars into the driveway.

"That was a brave man," Garine says as we step out. "He could have turned tail. He kept shooting until he

[151]

dropped." Leaving the car he half turns, and I see his left arm dripping blood.

"Hey!"

"It's nothing. Never touched the bone. And the bullet went clear through. So they missed this time!" He's right; there are two holes in his sleeve. "I had my hand on the back of the driver's seat. Trouble is, I'm bleeding like a pig. You want to go get Myroff?"

"Of course. Where is he?"

"The driver knows."

While the driver backs the car around, Garine mutters, "Maybe it's too bad."

I come back with Myroff. This skinny, blond, horse-faced doctor speaks only Russian at all well, so we don't talk. To nose into the driveway the driver has to scatter a ring of rubbernecks gaping at the corpse.

Garine's in his room. I wait in the little anteroom.

A quarter of an hour later, with his arm in a sling, he shows Myroff out, comes back, lies down across from me on the black wooden bunk, grimaces, fidgets, finds a comfortable spot, and settles. Where he lies, in shadow, all I can see of his face is sharp outlines: the straight line of his brows, the narrow bridge of his nose in highlight, the motion of his drooping mouth. "He's beginning to annoy me."

"Who? Myroff? Did he say it was serious?"

"This?" He shows me his arm. "I don't give a damn about this. No, he says I've got to—absolutely got to—get out of here." He shuts his eyes. "And the most annoying thing is, I think he's right."

"Then why stay?"

"It's complicated. Good God, these bunks are uncomfortable!" He stands up and then sits again on the low bunk, hunched forward as usual, elbow on his knee and chin in his hand. He considers. "This last while, I've had to think about my life fairly often. I was thinking about it again a few minutes ago, when Myroff was playing shaman. That fellow might not have missed me. You know, my life's a pretty forthright statement. But when I think about it that way, there's always one image, one memory that comes back to me."

"Yes. You told me in the hospital."

"No, not my trial, I don't think about my trial anymore. And what I'm talking about isn't something I *think* about; it's a memory deeper than memory. It was during the war, behind the lines. About fifty Legionnaires in a big room, a little light coming through a barred window. Raining outside. They've just lit candles stolen from a nearby church. One of them, dressed like a priest, is officiating at an altar made of crates covered with shirts. In front of him comes a sinister procession: a man in a frock coat with a huge paper flower in his buttonhole, a bride between two bridesmaids from some transvestite carnival act, and a lot of other weird characters in the shadows. Five o'clock. The candlelight's dim. I hear, 'Hold her up! Don't let little pussy pass out!' The bride's a young soldier who reported in yesterday from God knows where, and bragged that he'd bayonet the first man who made a pass at him. The two carnival bridesmaids pin him in place; he can hardly move, his eyelids are half shut, he's probably been beaten almost unconscious. The mayor takes the priest's place, they douse the candles, and all I can see then is men's backs humping in the deep shadow near the floor. The guy screams. Naturally they raped him until they were groggy. There were a lot of them. Yes. That's haunted me for a long time. Not because of the way it ended; because of the absurd parody that began it."

Again he muses. "It's not too different from what I felt during the trial. A remote but real connection."

He sweeps back the hair falling across his face and stands up, as if he wants to shake himself. The pin holding his sling in place pops open, and his arm falls; he bites his lips. While I search for the pin on the floor, he goes on slowly: "I have to be careful. When I become detached, when I seem to stand apart from my own actions, it's like losing blood. In the old days when I wasn't doing much of anything, I used to wonder what my life was worth. Now I know it's worth more than . . ."

He leaves the thought unfinished. I look up as I hand him the pin: the end of his sentence is a tight smile with pride in it—and a kind of bitter resentment. When our eyes meet he goes on, as if I'd called him back to the real world. "Where was I?"

I too have to grope: "You were telling me you think about your life often these days."

"Ah yes. It's like this. . . ."

He pauses again, waiting for the right words.

"It's always hard to talk about these things. Let's see. When I gave money to the midwives, you know perfectly well I had no illusions about the importance of 'the cause.' Still, I knew the risk, and I went ahead in spite of the warnings. All right. At the time I lost all my money I was letting myself go along with the system that was robbing me; and that loss had a good deal to do with bringing me here. My life is action, and I'm indifferent to everything that isn't action, including the results of action. I could tie myself to the revolution so easily because its outcome is remote and always shifting. Essentially I'm a gambler. Like all gamblers I only care about the game, stubbornly and passionately. I'm playing for bigger stakes these days than I used to, and I've learned how to play, but it's still the same game. And I know it inside out. There's a certain rhythm to my life, a personal destiny if you like, that I can't shake off. I hang on like grim death to whatever gives me strength. (I've also learned that a life isn't worth anything, but nothing is worth a life.) For a few days now I've felt that I'm forgetting what matters most; I have a hunch that something else is building up. I had a hunch about the trial, too, and losing my money. Well, what the hell! If we're going to wipe out Hong Kong, I'd like to . . ."

But he stops, stands up abruptly, winces, and murmurs, "Well, that's enough of that," and calls for the latest dispatches.

THE NEXT DAY

THE DECREE HAS BEEN ISSUED. We notified our Hong Kong groups immediately. And the advance guard of the red army, holding positions forty miles from the front, has just been ordered into the line. Nothing stands between us and full power but Ch'en Chiung-ming.

15 AUGUST

A holiday, in France. And not long ago, a feast day in the cathedral here. Now the cathedral's been transformed into a shelter for the poor, and it's guarded by red soldiers. Borodin had the government confiscate all religious buildings. Nothing in Europe can even suggest the misery of these masses, the misery of animals ravaged by some universal mange, gazing dimly out of dull, vacant eyes empty of appeal or even hate. At the sight of them a rude, equally animal resentment rises in me, compounded of shame, fear, and ignoble joy not to be one of them. Pity wells only when I'm out of sight of that emaciation, those mandrake's limbs, tatters, scabs big as a hand on that greenish skin, and those eyes already glassy and vague, scarcely human—when they aren't shut.

I talk to Garine about all that, in my turn.

"You don't have the habit of it," he answers. "The

memory of a certain level of poverty puts all things human in perspective; so does the idea of death. The best in Hong was born of that. So was the courage of the man who shot at me. Human beings swamped too deep in poverty never come out of it; they dissolve in it like lepers. But the others are the strongest tools for . . . minor dirty work, if not the most reliable. Courage, no notion of dignity, and plenty of hate.

"You remind me of something Lenin's supposed to have said, which Hong had tattooed on his arm—in English, deliberately: 'Will we inherit a world that hasn't bled to death?' He admired that fanatically at first; lately he's hated it just as fanatically. I think he left it there just out of hate."

"And because you can't erase a tattoo."

"Oh, he would've burned it off. He's a boy who hates with the whole heart."

"*Used to* hate."

He looks at me sadly: "Yes. Used to hate." And after a moment he adds, gazing at a palm leaf that lies across the window, "Is it true that for Lenin hope itself was that color?"

I look at his dark profile against the light. Seen so, he hasn't changed. And the profile, little different from when I arrived here almost two months ago, little different even from the one I knew years ago, is an emphatic contrast to the alteration in his voice. Since the night I saw him at the hospital he seems to have dissociated himself from his own actions, letting them drift away from him with his health, with his hold on life. What he just said still echoes in my mind: "The memory of a certain level of poverty puts all things human in perspective; so does the idea of death." He uses death often as a comparison now.

Propaganda's head of cinematography comes in. "Commissar, the new cameras are here from Vladivostok. And the films are ready. Do you want to see them?"

Instantly the tough, decisive expression returns to Garine's face. And he says, "Let's go," almost in his old tone of voice.

17 AUGUST

The red advance guard has just thrashed an enemy unit outside Wai-ch'ao. We retook the town: two artillery pieces, some machine guns, some tractors, and a large batch of prisoners fell into our hands. Three British prisoners who officered for Ch'en are already on the way to Canton. The houses of influential men who collaborated with enemy officers have been burned to the ground.

Ch'en is regrouping his forces; within a week the battle will begin. Propaganda's going all out now. The heads of public agencies and services are ordered to send all their men out pasting up posters and notices. There are posters or stickers below corrugated iron roofs, on wine shop windows, in every bar, in all public transportation, on rickshas, on pillars and columns in marketplaces, on the parapets of bridges, in every place of business: on the palm-leaf fans in barber shops, hung on bamboos in lantern shops, stuck to windows in bazaars, folded like fans in restaurant windows, taped to cars in garages. It's a game the whole city's playing. We see leaflets and posters everywhere, like newspapers in Europe every morning; rather small ones in the hands of passersby (the big ones are still being printed), with their superb victorious cadets and their Cantonese soldiers radiating beams of sunlight and watching haggard Englishmen and green Chinese flee; and at the bottom, smaller, a student, a peasant, a worker, a woman, and a soldier all hand in hand.

After siesta the good cheer turns to wild enthusiasm. Unbuttoned soldiers roister through the streets, everybody's outside, a dense crowd gathers along the riverside, solemn and tense in silent exaltation. Parades file through the streets with fifes, gongs and placards, followed by swarms of children. Bands of students march, brandishing little white flags that flutter, frothing and vanishing like sea spray above the robes and white suits packed together like an army. The dense, calm mass of the crowd inches along, opening to make way for parades and leaving a shaky wake behind where caps and Panama hats bob in upraised hands. On the walls our posters, and on the roofs immense placards hastily painted, translate the victory into pictures. In stifling heat, beneath a low white sky, the procession moves on, as if toward a temple. A number of aged Chinese women tag along with sleepy babies, hair beribboned, on their backs in black cloth slings. An uproar of gongs, firecrackers, shouts, and musical instruments rises from the streets together with the vague shuffling of innumerable feet and the muted clack of innumerable wooden sandals. The acrid dust dances as high as a man, rasping my throat, and subsides in drifting eddies in the narrow, almost deserted side streets, where only a few latecomers rush along, uncomfortable in their holiday best. Almost all the shops' shutters are half open or closed altogether, as on great holidays.

I've never felt as keenly as today the isolation Garine mentioned to me, the solitude we live in, the distance between our own fundamental natures and this crowd's actions, even its enthusiasm.

THE NEXT DAY

Garine comes back from Borodin's furious. "I don't say he's wrong to use Klein's murder, just as he'd use anything else. What I thought was stupid, what really got my dander up, was his gall, ordering me to make a speech at Klein's grave. There are plenty of good speakers around. But no! He's still a slave to that insufferable Bolshevik mentality, that moronic glorification of discipline. Well, that's his business. But I didn't toss Europe away like a ragbag just to wind up like some Rebecci; not to come out here and teach obedience and not to learn it either. 'There are no half-measures in the revolution!' Balls. There are half-measures wherever there're men and not machines. He wants to mass-produce revolutionaries the way Ford turns out cars! There's going to be trouble, and sooner than you think. In that hairy Mongol's head of his the Bolshevik's battling the Jew, and if the Bolshevik wins, so much the worse for the Comintern."

A pretext. That's not the reason for their quarrel at all.

There's another reason first: Borodin had Hong executed. I think Garine wanted to save him. In spite of the murder of the hostages (and anyway that doesn't seem to have been done on Hong's orders). Because he thought Hong was still useful; because there's a kind of feudal bond between Garine and his men. And maybe because he was sure that Hong would wind up on his side, if necessary, against Borodin. Which seems to have been Borodin's opinion too.

Garine believes only in energy. He's not anti-Marxist, but Marxism isn't a "scientific socialism" to him at all; it's a way to organize the workers' emotions, a way to recruit shock troops among the proletariat. Patiently Borodin is building the ground floor of a Communist edifice. He reproaches Garine for a lack of perspective, for not knowing where he's headed, for winning random victories— however brilliant and necessary they may be. Already, in his eyes, Garine belongs to the past.

Garine agrees that Borodin's following a carefully considered program, but Garine thinks it's a bad program, that Borodin's narrow-minded communism is bound to produce a right-wing Kuomintang opposition much stronger than Ch'eng-tai's that will crush the workers' militia.

And he's discovered (late in the day) that communism, like all powerful doctrines, is a freemasonry. That in the name of discipline Borodin wouldn't hesitate to replace Garine as soon as they could do without him; replace him by a man less expert, perhaps, but more obedient.

When the decree was announced in Hong Kong, the British held a meeting at the Grand Theater and telegraphed London again demanding a British expeditionary force. The reply too came by telegraph: the British government is opposed to any military intervention.

We've recorded the interrogation of the captured British officers, and records have been sent to all units. But every officer denied flatly that he'd come out to fight us on orders from his government; we had to delete that passage. We'll have to cut much more *instructive* records. Garine says people question a newspaper story but never a picture or a sound, and at first the only way to fight propaganda by phonograph and movies is with propaganda by phonograph and movies; and the enemy propaganda people, even the British, don't know how to do that yet.

"He's doing great things before he leaves," Nikolaieff said to me this morning. "He" being Garine.

"Before he leaves?"

"Yes, I think this time he's really on his way."

"He's been on his way every week."

"Yes, yes, but this time he'll go, you watch. He's made up his mind. If England had sent troops, I think he'd have stayed; but he knows London's answer. I think he's only waiting to see who wins the next battle. Myroff says he'll never even reach Ceylon."

"And why not?"

"Very simply, young man, because he's on his last legs."

"Anybody can say that."

"It's not anybody saying it, it's Myroff."

"He could be wrong too."

"Seems it isn't only malaria and dysentery. Tropical diseases, you know, you don't fool around with them, young fellow. When you've got one, you take care of yourself. If not, you pay for it. And maybe it's just as well."

"Not for him!"

"His day is over. Men like him were needed, sure, but now the red army's on the march, and Hong Kong'll be brought to its knees in a few days: now we need men who don't think quite so much of themselves. I have nothing against him, believe me. I can work with him or with anybody. Still, he has his prejudices. I don't hold it against him, but he has." Squinting, with a lopsided smile: "Human, all too human, as Borodin says. That's where disease takes you if you don't stop to treat it."

I think of Ling's interrogation, of Garine's objections that Nikolaieff calls prejudices.

He shuts up for a while, then lays a heavy finger on my chest and goes on: "He's not a communist, that's all. I don't give a damn myself, but all the same Borodin is logical: there's no room in communism for people who . . . well, insist on being themselves, existing apart from the others."

"Does communism oppose individual conscience?"

"It demands more. Individualism is a bourgeois sickness."

"But at Propaganda we've seen how right Garine is. To give up your individualism here is to invite defeat. And

[161]

everybody who works with us, Russian or not—except Borodin, maybe—is as much an individualist as he is."

"You know they just had a serious quarrel, Borodin and Garine, or at least people say it was serious. Ah, Borodin!" He shoves his hands into his pockets and smiles with a touch of hostility: "There's a lot could be said about him."

"If the ancient Romans in the party—let me call them that, the ones consolidating the revolution in Moscow—if they can't accept the kind of revolutionaries who are, well, what? *conquerors*, who are about to win China for them, then they'll——"

"Conquerors? Your friend Garine would find the word bitter."

"—put a dangerous limit to——"

"But it's not important. You don't understand the first thing about it. Rightly or wrongly, Borodin's staking all he can on whatever stands for the proletariat here. His first duty is to that proletariat, a sort of nucleus, that has to learn what it is and grow enough to seize power. Borodin's a kind of navigator who——"

"Garine too. He doesn't think he made this revolution all alone!"

"But Borodin knows his ship, and Garine doesn't know his. As Borodin says, 'He has no true north.' "

"Except the revolution."

"You talk like a little boy. The revolution's true north only as long as it's unfinished. Otherwise it wouldn't be a revolution but a simple coup d'état, or a pronunciamento. Sometimes I wonder if he won't end up following Mussolini. Do you know Pareto?"

"No."

"Garine must know him."

"But you're forgetting one thing. Even if his positive reasons are what you say they are (and that's not true), his negative reasons are obvious: a solid hatred of the bourgeoisie and all it stands for. And negative drives can count for a lot."

"True, true, a White general—leading the Reds. That's OK as long as we're fighting the common enemy: Britain. (There's good reason why he's running Propaganda for the Kuomintang.) But afterward? When it comes to organizing a country, if he bets on communism he'll have to become another Borodin; if he bets on democracy— and that would surprise me, the Kuomintang leaders disgust him—he's all washed up: he won't want to spend his life in cloakroom politics with Chinese ward heelers, and he can't take a chance on a dictatorship. He'd fail at that because he's not Chinese. So he's just as well off going back to Europe and dying there in peace and glory. The time for men like him is just about over. Communism can still use that kind of revolutionary (he's really a 'specialist' here), but only with a tough Chekist on either side of him. Tough. What's the sense of this halfway police state? Borodin, Garine, all that . . ." With his languid gesture he seems to be mixing liquids.

"Ever since I met Garine, the deep thinkers have been predicting his future," Nikolaieff goes on. "And Borodin will end up the same as your friend: individual conscience is the real disease of leaders. What we miss most around here is a real Cheka."

10 P.M.

The soft lapping of ripples, the bang of junks bumping. Hidden behind the roof, the moon brightens the clear, warm night. Two suitcases against the wall on the veranda: Garine's decided to leave tomorrow morning. He's been meditating for quite a while, eyes empty, arms relaxed. When I get up to find a red pencil and make notes on the *Canton Gazette* I've been reading, he comes out of his trance: "I was thinking again of what my father said, 'You must never let go of the land.' Living in one absurd world or another . . . There's no power, not even any *real life*, without a conviction of the world's futility—an obsession with it."

I know the whole meaning of his own life is tied to that belief; I know he draws great strength from his deep feeling that human existence is absurd. If the world isn't absurd, then he's frittered away his life in vain gestures— not in a fundamental, exalting vanity but in the vanity of despair. Hence the need to impose his beliefs. But tonight everything within me resists him; I'm arguing against his truth echoing in myself, a truth that his imminent death reinforces ominously. What I feel is less protest than rebellion. He waits for my answer like an enemy.

"What you say may be true. But the way you say it makes it false, absolutely false. If you live this real life to fight that . . . other life, you can't do it full of private yearnings and private resentments."

"What resentments?"

"There's plenty here to hold a man who's proved his strength the way you have, plenty——"

"To know your own strength is even worse."

"—to bind him for life, for——"

"I'm counting on you to set an example!" He answers with an almost vindictive irony. Neither of us speaks for a time. I suddenly want to say something to bring us closer; I'm childishly afraid to see our friendship end, to part this way from a man I've loved, a man I still love, whatever he says and whatever he thinks, a man about to die.

But again he's stronger than I am. He lays his right hand on my arm and says, in a slow, affectionate voice, "No, listen, I'm not trying to be right. I'm not trying to persuade you. I'm just being true to myself. I've seen many

[164]

men suffer. Many, many men and sometimes abjectly, sometimes horribly. I'm not soft, but I've been moved to the most profound pity, an agonizing, choking pity. When I was alone with myself again, that pity always drained away. Suffering tends to prove the absurdity of life, not to throw doubt on it; suffering shows how silly life is. At times Klein's life fills me with something like— like—"

He hesitates not because he's groping for the right words, but because he finds it hard to say them. Then he goes on, looking me in the eye: "All right then, like a certain kind of laughter. Do you understand? People don't react sensibly when their lives don't make sense. Walled-in lives, where the world's reflected like funny-faces in a distorting mirror. Maybe it shows its true face somewhere in there, but that doesn't matter: nobody— nobody, you understand?—can tolerate that face. You can live accepting the absurd, you can't live *in* the absurd. People who want to 'let go of the land' find it sticking to their fingers. You can't escape it, but you can't find it by looking for it." He hammers his thigh with a fist. "The only way to fight back is to create something. Borodin says what men like me create alone can't last. As if what men like him create—ah, would I like to see this China five years from now! What lasts, that's what matters!"

Another silence.

"Why didn't you leave sooner?"

"Why leave as long as you can do something else?"

"Simple prudence."

He shrugs, and after another pause says, "You can't live by private fears."

Another silence.

"And the beast sinks its claws into us anyway."

He falls silent. A strange, indefinable, vague sound rises, I can't tell where from, far off and muffled. He too cocks

[165]

an ear. But we hear the soft crackle of tires on gravel: a cyclist has just ridden into the courtyard. The sharp clack of footsteps approaches. Announced by the boy, a messenger brings in two envelopes.

Garine opens the first and passes it to me: CH'EN CHIUNG-MING'S ENTIRE ARMY IS IN ACTION AGAINST ALL RED ARMY UNITS NOW AT THE FRONT. The decisive battle has begun.

While I'm reading, he opens the second, shrugs, crumples it into a ball, and tosses it away. "I don't give a damn. I don't give a damn now. Let them work it out."

The messenger leaves. We hear his steps receding, the gate clanging shut. But Garine's changed his mind: standing at the window, he's calling him back.

The gate again. The messenger returns. Standing beneath the window, he talks to Garine, but Garine is coughing and I can't make out the words.

The courier leaves again. Garine paces the room, angry now.

"What is it?"

"Nothing!"

Obviously. He picks up the ball of paper, unfolds it, and smooths it—not easy with his left arm immobilized. Then he turns to me. "Let's go!" As we dash downstairs he mutters—to himself or to me?—"A good way to kill off ten thousand men!" I ask no questions, so he decides to go on: "Two of our own men, Propaganda agents, taken at one of the wells our troops use, with cyanide in their pockets. Double agents. No reason to be in the area. Said nothing, confessed nothing. And Nikolaieff tells me he'll proceed with the interrogation tomorrow!"

He's driving the car himself, flat out; the driver's asleep. Garine says nothing more. He steers with his good hand and twice we almost jump the curb. He slows down, gives me the wheel, and then seems to forget me, his head turtled down between his shoulders—his cheeks, hollower than ever, flash briefly every time we pass a street light.

In the corridor at police headquarters I notice the huge pink posters—I'd half-seen them just now in the streets: the decree, all over town thanks to us.

When we reach Nikolaieff's office, the military clack of our heels, sinister in the silence, announcing us, Nikolaieff is sitting behind his desk like a hearty peasant, leaning well back in his chair, his tiny pig eyes on the two prisoners. They're both in blue linen dockworkers' outfits. One has a silky, drooping black mustache; the other is an old man with a crew cut, and shining eyes lively in his round face.

I'm growing used to these nighttime hours at Propaganda and police headquarters, the silence, the sickly-sweet smell of flowers, mud, and gasoline fumes in the hot night, and our own drawn, tense faces, gummy eyelids, hunched shoulders, slack mouths—and on our tongues the depressing taste of a hangover.

"Any news of the battle?" Garine asks as he enters.

"Nothing. They're still at it."

"And your two buddies here?"

"You got my note. That's all I know. So far, anyway. Can't get a word out if them. It'll come."

"Who vouched for them?"

"N-72, according to the report."

"Check on it. If it's true, N-72 has to be brought in, tried in a hurry by the special court, and executed."

"You know he's one of our best agents—"

Garine looks down his nose.

"—and he's done great things for me. Often. He's loyal."

"He won't have to bother to be, anymore. And I've had more than enough of his services. Got that?"

The other smiles and nods his sleepy head once, look-

[167]

ing like the porcelain Buddha he's set ironically on his desk.

"Now for these two."

I pull out notebook and pen.

"No, no need to write it down, it won't take that long. And Nikolaieff will jot down the answers. Now: who gave you the poison?"

The first prisoner, the younger, launches a silly story: he was ordered to hand over the packet to someone whose name he didn't know, a woman who would have his description, but . . .

Garine understands fairly well; all the same, I translate sentence by sentence. As if he had a tic, the Chinese touches his open hand to the long brushes of his mustache, then withdraws the hand nervously, realizing that the gesture muffles his voice; then touches again. Wearily Nikolaieff stares up at the buggy light bulb and smokes. The fans are off; the smoke drifts straight up.

"Enough," Garine says. His hand goes to his belt. "Swell! Forgot it again!" He opens my holster with his good hand, pulls my revolver, and lays it on the desk; the metal gleams. "Tell the first one very precisely that if he hasn't told us what we want to know within five minutes, I'll shoot him in the head myself."

I translate. Nikolaieff shrugs almost imperceptibly: all our spies know that Garine is a "great leader" and his approach here is childish. One minute . . . two . . .

"That's enough. Tell him to answer up."

"You told him he could have five minutes," Nikolaieff says, ironically respectful.

"You go to hell," Garine says. He's picked up the revolver. The weight of the weapon steadies his right hand; his left, hanging from the sling, trembles feverishly. Again I tell the Chinese to answer. He gestures helplessly.

The shot explodes. The Chinese doesn't budge; on his

face is a look of intense astonishment. Nikolaieff jumps in his chair, and leans back against the wall. Is the prisoner hurt?

A second . . . two . . . The Chinese collapses, inert, legs askew. And the blood begins to flow.

Nikolaieff stammers, "But . . . but . . ."

"Go to hell!" Garine's tone silences the fat man, who's not smiling now; his mouth has fallen open, exaggerating his jowls. His fat hands are crossed on his chest in an old woman's gesture. Garine stares at the wall; from the lowered barrel a wisp of transparent smoke rises.

"The other one now. Translate again."

Unnecessary. Terrified, his eyes rolling, the old man's already talking. Nikolaieff grabs a pencil and takes notes with an unsteady hand.

"Shut up," Garine says in Cantonese. He turns to me: "Warn him before he goes on that if he lies, he's in big trouble."

"He knows it."

"If necessary the execution can be refined."

"How do you want me to tell him that?"

"Any way you like."

(And he seems to understand.)

While the prisoner gasps out his story, Nikolaieff blows away the mayflies fallen on his notes.

The man was paid by Ch'en Chiung-ming's agents, that much is obvious. He talks fast at first but doesn't say much that's important; seeing the pistol lowered, he hesitates. Abruptly, he falls silent. Exasperated, Garine glares.

"And if . . . if I tell you everything, what will you give——"

He goes down hard, his arms out like flippers, and skids a few feet. A furious Garine has just slugged him on the jaw; fist still clenched, Garine frowns, gnaws at his lips, and sits on a corner of the desk. "My wound broke open." The prisoner is playing dead on the floor. "Ask him if he ever heard anybody talk about incense." Again I translate. The man opens his eyes slowly and says, without standing up, looking at us, or talking to anybody in particular, "There were three. Two are captured. One of the two is dead. The other is alive. The third one may be over by the wells."

Garine and I look at Nikolaieff, who was going to postpone the rest of the interrogation until tomorrow. He works hard to conceal emotion; his mouth and brows are still, but his cheeks go taut and slack, as if they were trembling. He takes notes while the prisoner goes into detail.

"That's all?"

"Yes."

"If you've left anything out . . ."

"I've told you everything." Now the prisoner seems indifferent.

Nikolaieff rings, shows us a sheet of paper, then gives it to the orderly. "A bike to the special telegraph office. Urgent." He turns back to us: "Under the circumstances . . . under the circumstances . . . there may be others, you know . . . so . . . Garine . . . you don't think we ought to work him over a little, just in case?"

To win a pardon for his own criminal negligence he's ready—this one, who wanted to postpone the interrogation until tomorrow—to torture the man "just in case."

"A one-track mind," Garine mutters. Then louder, "So he can tell us lies and start us down false trails? He can't have any general information. In the work at the wells there's hardly ever more than three agents. Three, you hear? Not two!"

Now he rings, four times. Two soldiers come in and march the prisoner out. Nikolaieff makes no answer, but brushes gently at the mayflies still falling on his desk, as if he were smoothing his notes with a schoolboy's careful gesture.

In the corridor we run into an orderly from the Commissariat for War, bearing a dispatch: Ch'en's troops have begun to give ground.

The stairway of Garine's house, pitch black: the bulb is shattered. Night lies heavy, outside and in my nerves. My eyelids are burning but I'm not sleepy. My body shivers gently, as if I were getting drunk; as I climb ponderously, groping for each step with my toes, my eyes close and I see distorted images, now murky and now strangely sharp: the two prisoners, the dead prisoner on the floor, Nikolaieff, the grotesque wedding Garine told me about, the flashing streetlights, Klein's gashed face, the pink bloom of posters. I shudder, as if I were waking with a start, when I hear Garine's voice: "I can't get used to this darkness. It always makes me feel like a blind man."

But light glows; we're in the small room again; the two valises are still there.

"Is that all you're taking?"

"For a few months, it's enough."

But he's hardly paying attention. He's listening carefully to a very faint sound that fills the whole house. I was wondering about it before we left.

"You hear that?"

"Yes. I heard it before."

"Where do you think it's coming from?"

"Listen."

There's something mysterious about the smothered, distant, mechanical sound. It's a muffled gnashing like nibbling rats, but regular and rhythmic. Noises like the snapping of dried wood seem to break the surface now

[171]

and then, like bubbles in turgid waters; they rumble briefly like all the other sounds in the night, and are absorbed then by the constant grinding creak that seems to come from the cellar and the sky at the same time. Garine is uneasy, barely breathing, tense, making as little noise as possible. The creak of his shoes silences those odd sounds brutally; after a few seconds they revive like a feeble gleam, then swell again to their remote and inexplicable intensity. Finally he lets himself relax, gestures his indifference, and lies down on the wooden bunk. "Want some coffee while we wait?"

"No thanks. You'd do better to take some quinine and change that dressing."

"Plenty of time." He glances at his suitcases. "Three months, maybe six . . . ?" Still preoccupied, he nibbles at the inside of his cheek. "Well, I suppose it wouldn't be very smart to stay here because I didn't leave in time." When he says "stay" he doesn't mean "remain," but "die." "My old friend Nikolaieff's been hinting it's already sort of late." So far he's been talking to himself. Now his tone alters; he shrugs his good shoulder. "What a dummy! If I hadn't chased back there tonight . . . Who can Borodin find to replace me? Chen, for distribution, but what about the other branches? With a few more heroes like Nikolaieff—disciplined, strictly disciplined—it could all end in disaster. Klein is dead. What shape will they be in when I come back? One little blunder at police headquarters, and I slip back into Cantonese life the way I slip into my jacket; and even so I feel as if I'd already left. I tell you! If I die at sea, they'll be able to paste some pretty label on the bag!"

His lips are even thinner now, and his eyes are shut. The shadow of his prominent nose merges with the pouch below his left eye. He's ugly, with the sharp, unnerving ugliness of the dead, before serenity settles upon them.

"To think that when I first arrived, in Lambert's day, Canton was a comic-opera republic! And today—England! To conquer a city. To bring a city to its knees. The city is man's most social creation, it stands for society itself, and there's at least one that the scruffy Cantonese are whipping into shape! That decree. All that hard work, by all those people, transforming Hong Kong into a clenched fist, is finally . . ." He lowers his feet to the floor and sits forward slowly, heavily, as if he were crushing something. He sits straighter then and pulls a small, round, celluloid-backed mirror from his pocket. He stares at his own face. It's the first time I've seen him do that.

"I think it's time, all right. Be pretty damn foolish to die here like some colonial type. If people like me aren't assassinated, who will be?"

Something in what he says disturbs me, makes me uneasy. He goes on: "What the hell can I do in Europe, though? Moscow? The way things stand between Borodin and me . . . I don't trust the Comintern's methods, but we'll have to wait and see. . . . In six days, Shanghai; then the Norwegian ship and that sense of stepping into the lobby. I only hope I don't find everything I've done shot to pieces when I get back here. Borodin has plenty of drive, but he can be plenty clumsy too at times. Ah, we never go where we'd like to go!"

"All right, where would you like to go?"

"England. Now I know what the British Empire is. Stubborn, unrelenting force. Running things. Making decisions. Controlling men. That's where life is."

And I see suddenly why his words upset me: it isn't me he's trying to persuade. He doesn't believe in what he's saying and he's trying hard, with every raw nerve, to persuade himself. Does he know he's doomed? Is he only afraid he's doomed? Or doesn't he know anything for sure? In the presence of certain death a melancholy annoyance at his chatter, his hopes, flares up inside me. I feel like telling him, "Enough! Enough! You are going to die!" A wild impulse tempts me, but face to face with him the sheer physical impossibility of it calms me down. Disease has wasted his face to the point where I can easily imagine him dead. And I know that if I mentioned death, I'd be attacking him with his own image, with the gaunt features that haunt me. And it's as if there'd be something dangerous in what I said, as if my words would confirm his own foreknowledge of death.

He's been silent for several moments. And in this new silence, again we hear the mysterious rumbling that intrigued us a while ago. It's not a rumble now but the sound of one jolt after another, very distant or very muffled, a sound out of a dream; as if someone's tamping the earth, far away, with heavy objects cushioned by felt. And the sharper sounds, like the sounds of snapping wood, become metallic. It brings to mind the roaring of a forge beneath the musical clang of hammers. . . .

And once again the crunch of tires on gravel adds to the mingling noises. A cadet comes upstairs, announced by a boy. He brings an answer from the telegraph officer. The sound, though distant, fills the room.

"Do you hear it?" Garine asks the boy.

"Yes, Commissar."

"What is it?"

"Don't know, Commissar."

The cadet nods. "It's the army, Comrade Garine."

Garine stares at him.

" The red army's rear guard moving up to the line."

Garine takes a deep breath, then reads the dispatches and passes them to me:

THIRD AGENT CAPTURED CARRYING 800 GRAMS CYANIDE. ENEMY ROUTED. SEVERAL REGIMENTS INFILTRATED BY PROPAGANDA COME OVER TO US. STORES AND ARTILLERY IN

OUR HANDS. HEADQUARTERS DISORGANIZED. CAVALRY PUR-
SUING CH'EN WHO IS IN FULL FLIGHT.

He signs the receipt and hands it back to the cadet, who follows the boy out.

"He won't see my signature again for a while! Ch'en's troops cut to ribbons . . . in another year, Shanghai . . ."

The faint rumble of the marching troops surges and ebbs with the warm wind. Now we recognize the clatter of tractors, the ground trembling under the pounding tramp of marching men, and at intervals, wafted in on a stifling gust, a quick tattoo of hoofbeats or the metallic clank of gun carriages. With that distant uproar a puzzling exaltation seems to fill him. Is it joy?

"I probably won't see you tomorrow morning, with all those damn fools down there to say good-bye. . . ."

Biting down on his lower lip, he works his wounded arm slowly free of the sling and stands up. We embrace. A strange melancholy blooms, a deep desperate sadness at the futility of life and the presence of death. . . . When the light strikes our faces again, he gazes at me. In his eyes I look for the joy I thought I saw; but I find nothing of the kind, only a tough yet fraternal gravity.

AFTERWORD

1949

Over twenty years have passed since the publication of this young man's novel, and much water has flowed under how many broken bridges! Twenty years after the capture of Peking by Chiang Kai-shek's revolutionary army, we await the capture of Chiang Kai-shek's Canton by Mao Tse-tung's revolutionary army. In twenty years will another revolutionary army drive out the "fascist" Mao? What does the shade of Borodin think of all this, Borodin who when last heard of, before the war, was petitioning the Kremlin for "a lodging with a fireplace"? And the shade of Galen, a suicide?

And yet, despite the complicated interplay that has perhaps —perhaps—cast China on Russia's side, Mao's troops have plucked their victories from the revolt that inspired other troops in 1925. It is not the old passion for liberation that has altered. What has altered most is not China and not Russia, but Europe: out there Europe has ceased to matter.

But this book bears only superficially on history. If it has survived it's not because it depicted certain episodes of the Chinese revolution, but because it portrayed a certain type of hero who combined culture, logic, and a talent for action. Those values were indirectly linked to the values of Europe at the time. And as I am now asked, "What has become of intellectual values in today's Europe?" I prefer to answer with the appeal I made to intellectuals on 5 March 1948 at the Salle Pleyel in Paris, on behalf of my Gaullist colleagues.

Its form—the transcript of a speech improvised from notes— shows only too well that this is no carefully tooled essay. Certain of the ideas expressed here have been developed on another level in *The Voices of Silence*. But the element of breathless preaching inevitable in a prepared speech seemed better reserved to the novel's passions (and the novel's limits), and not superimposed on a pretended objectivity. The decay of European consciousness is only summarily analyzed here.

The problem was to focus on the most immediate, and at the same time the most insidious, threat: dehumanization by means of psychological techniques (propaganda has come a long way since Garine); and to specify what, in our opinion, must be PRESERVED.

The European spirit is the object of a double metamorphosis. As we see it, the drama of the twentieth century is this: simultaneously the political myth of the International is dying and an unprecedented internationalization of culture is proceeding inexorably.

Throughout the last century, from Michelet's mighty voice to Juarez's mighty voice, there seemed to be serious evidence that in shattering the bonds of nationality we became more human. That was neither baseness nor error: it was the shape of hope. Victor Hugo thought that the United States of Europe would develop effortlessly and would foreshadow the United States of the World. But the United States of Europe will be born in travail, and the United States of the World is a long way off. . . .

What we have learned is that Russia's grand, scornful gesture in discarding its anthem, the "Internationale" (which will always be linked to Russia, whether she likes it or not, in mankind's eternal dream of justice), sweeps away the dreams of the nineteenth century at one stroke. We know now that in becoming less French we do not become more human, only more Russian. For better or for worse, we are tied to the nation. And we know that we shall not create the European without her; that willy-nilly we must create the European upon her.

As that immense hope died, as each man was flung back upon his homeland, a flood of new works burst upon civilization: music and the plastic arts had invented their printing press. Translations crossed borders freely; Colonel Lawrence sat side by side with Benjamin Constant; the Payot series, with the Garnier Foreign Classics.

And finally the cinema was born. At this very moment a Hindu woman watching *Anna Karenina* may burst into tears seeing a Swedish actress and an American director express the Russian Tolstoi's idea of love.

If we haven't reconciled the dreams of the living, at least we've bound the dead closer!

And in this hall tonight we can say without embarrassment, "You gathered here are the first generation of mankind to inherit the entire earth."

How is such a legacy possible? We note carefully that every vanished civilization appealed to only a part of man. That of the Middle Ages was primarily a culture of the soul; that of the eighteenth century, a culture of the mind. From age to age successive civilizations, appealing to successive elements in man, were superimposed; they were properly fused only for their inheritors. Inheritance is always metamorphosis. The true heir to Chartres is of course not the art of Saint Sulpice,* but Rembrandt. Michelangelo, striving to remake antiquity, made Michelangelo.

What would our civilization's ancestors have had to say to one another? It combines a Greek element, a Roman, a Biblical, we all know that; but what would have passed between Caesar and the prophet Elijah? Insults. For the true birth of a dialogue between Christ and Plato, Montaigne had to be born.

Only in the inheritor comes the metamorphosis from which life springs.

And who lays claim to that metamorphosis today? The United States, the Soviet Union, Europe. Let's clear the

* A church in Paris rebuilt several times, now a hodge-podge of styles and modifications, from the antique to murals by Delacroix. (Tr.)

ground a bit before we go on to the essential problem, and let's discard the foolish notion that cultures are in constant conflict, as countries are. Latin America alone proves how silly that is. In our own time she is in the process of reconciling—without a pitched battle—what she wants to take from the Anglo-Saxon world and what she wants to take from the Latin world. There are irreducible political differences; but it is absolutely not true that cultural conflicts are by definition irreducible. They may be, and most dangerously; or they may not be at all.

Let's also spare ourselves that ridiculous Manichaeism, that distinction between the speaker's friends, angels, and the speaker's enemies, devils, which has come into fashion when America and Russia are the topic. What we think of Russian policy toward our own country is obvious: we think that the same forces that made her France's ally at the Liberation have made her France's implacable adversary since; and we intend to do something about that. But Stalin doesn't diminish Dostoevski, any more than Moussorgsky's genius guarantees Stalin's politics.

Let's look first at the American claim to the world's cultural heritage. First point: there is no culture in America which defines itself as specifically American. That's a European invention. In America one feels that there is a characteristic context to life. One feels that America is a rootless country, an urban country, a country unaware of the ancient and profound connection with trees and stones common to the most ancient spirits of China and the most ancient spirits of the Occident. A country with the great advantage over us of being able to, and wanting to, welcome all the world's heritages with equal fervor; and a country in which any major museum displays, in the same hall, Romanesque statues gazing off at our Occident, and T'ang statues gazing off at Chinese civilization.

But a superior antiquarian's warehouse, even on an epic scale, is not a great culture. And the moment we set aside Europe's influence, American culture is a realm of acquired knowledge infinitely more than a realm of organic culture.

Furthermore, the mass arts—radio, films, the press— are now picking up an American accent everywhere.

Its art seems specifically American to us when it's an art of the masses. And there's not really that much difference between the spirit of *Life* magazine and the spirit of *Samedi Soir*; it's just that there are more Americans than there are Frenchmen.

And finally, America possesses a characteristic romanticism. But again, is it specifically American? Incontestably there is an American way of looking at the world which eternally reduces that world to its romantic version. But must I remind you that in *The Three Musketeers* Richelieu is important not for his influence on France but because he warns that Anne of Austria's diamond studs, gift of the King, are missing? For the moment America represents the romantic more than any country, but probably because she is a country of masses. And culture ranges far beyond such questions. What do cultivated Americans think? They think that American culture is one of the national cultures of the Western world, that there is no more difference between high American culture and high French culture than between the latter and high English culture, or what high German culture used to be. We Europeans aren't all that much alike! And believe me, the distance from Bergsonism to behaviorism is of the same order as the distance from Hegel to Bergson. In short, relative to us America has never seen herself, on the cultural plane, as a discrete part of the world; *she has always seen herself as part of* our *world*. There's not so much an American art, as American artists. We live by the same value systems; they don't reflect everything essential from Europe's past, but everything in them that's essential is linked to Europe. I repeat: an American culture, as distinct from our own as Chinese culture, is purely and simply a European invention.

And there are no specifically American cultural assumptions in conflict with our own except precisely insofar as Europe has abdicated its beliefs and responsibilities.

It's hard to be altogether comfortable with the idea of Russia as a European country.

St. Petersburg used to give us (and Leningrad still does) the impression of a European "settlement," a vast imperial branch of the Occident—shops, barracks, and cupolas—a New Delhi of the north.

But to take the Russians for Asiatics, and therefore for a kind of Chinese or Hindus, as their enemies always have, is ridiculous. The truth may be that we ought not to take maps too seriously, and that Russia is neither in Europe nor in Asia (it's in Russia), as Japan, where love and the army are so important, is neither in China nor in America.

The other countries of Europe share its culture on many levels and by way of exchanges. In one century or another Italy, Spain, France, and England have predominated. Those countries have much in common: the cultural myth of Greece and Rome, and the heritage of fifteen centuries of a common Christianity. That last heritage, which itself separates the Slavs of Bohemia from the Slavs of Russia, is surely an important influence; and the heritage of Byzantium is so influential in Russia that Russian painting has never worked free of it, and Stalin invokes Basil II at least as often as Peter the Great.

Russia entered Western culture in the nineteenth century, with her composers and novelists. And at that, Dostoevski is probably the only one of their novelists to consider himself distinctly Russian.

Ilya Ehrenburg commented indirectly on an interview I gave about Atlantic civilization, by asking, "Which is European, the atomic bomb or Tolstoi?"

If it's all right with you, we won't bother with the atomic bomb tonight. If the Russians had none then, it wasn't for lack of trying. And to urge Stalin on us as a man of Gandhi's sort, doesn't make much sense.

There remains Tolstoi. Which Tolstoi? The author of *Anna Karenina* and *War and Peace* isn't simply a European, but one of the giants of the Western spirit. The old warning goes, "Don't spit where you drink." When he wrote his novels he willed himself European, and felt that he was Balzac's rival in particular. But if we're talking about the Count Lev Nikolaevich who tried to live like a Gandhian Christian, who died in the snow like a Sunday-supplement hero, who wrote that he "preferred a good pair of boots to Shakespeare," then I think of the great Byzantine visionaries—and if I absolutely had to compare him to another genius, it would be Tagore, inseparable from India and writing in *The Home and the World* one of the great universal novels; it would not be Stendhal.

What most separates him from us is doubtless what also separates us from Russia: his Oriental dogmatism. Stalin believes in his own truth, and there is no free play in that truth; but Tolstoi, when he divorced himself from the West, believed no less in his own truth; and Dostoevski's genius was at the service of his implacable preaching all his life. Russia never had a Renaissance, nor an Athens; nor a Bacon, nor a Montaigne.

In Russia there's always been an urge toward Sparta and an urge toward Byzantium. Sparta integrates itself smoothly with the Occident; Byzantium, no. In the frenzied industrialization of that immense country, under way for thirty years now, we can see the most furious drive to westernize since Peter the Great. "Catch up with America! Pass her!" But the greater that effort, the harder the Russian spirit resists.

It's no accident that the Russian communists are attacking Picasso. His painting throws doubt on the fundamentals of their system; it is willy-nilly a most intensely European presence.

In the realm of the intellect everything that Russia calls formalism, that she has deported or tirelessly liquidated for the past ten years, is Europe. Suspected painters, writers, filmmakers, philosophers are above all suspected of submitting to the influence of a "degenerate Europe." Europeans, Eisenstein, Babel, Prokofiev! The spirit of Europe is a danger to a Pharaonic industry. Moscow's rebuke to Picasso is no accident: it represents a defense of the five-year plans. ...

Depending on whether an artist dies in time, or a little too late, he's buried with honors in the Kremlin wall or without honor at the foot of a wall in a Siberian prison camp.

The real reason why Russia is not European has nothing to do with geography. It's the Russian will.

I'm not giving a course here in the history of culture. I'm talking about Europe only in relation to the Soviet Union and the United States. Europe shows two characteristics at the moment:

The first is the link between art and culture. Those two realms are kept separate in Russia by a general dogmatism of thought. They are no less irreducibly separated in the United States, because in the United States the man of culture is not the artist, he is a university man. An American writer—Hemingway, Faulkner—isn't at all the equivalent of Gide or Valéry, but the equivalent of Rouault or Braque. They are dazzling specialists within a systematic culture of systematic knowledge; they are neither men of history nor ideologues.

The second point, important in another way: the will to transcend, to survive. Careful! Europe is the part of the world where Chartres, Michelangelo, Shakespeare, and Rembrandt lived in succession. Do we repudiate them, yes or no? No! Then we have to know what we're talking about.

We seem to think of ourselves as poor unfortunates, facing one immense culture called American novelists and another immense culture called I'm not too sure what —at best, Russian composers (which is incidentally not bad).

Yet the whole world still looks to Europe ultimately, and Europe alone can answer its most profound questions. Then who took Michelangelo's place? The glow they seek in Europe is the last glow of Rembrandt's light; and Europe's grand, tremulous gesture in what she thinks is her death agony is still the heroic gesture of Michelangelo....

They've just reproached us: "Those are bourgeois values." But why this definition of art by its context?

Understand me well. I see justice in a Russian philosopher—shipped to Siberia since, by the way—saying that "Plato's thought is inseparable from slavery." It's true that there's a historical setting to thought, a social conditioning of thought. But the problem doesn't end there; it begins there. You, for example, you've read Plato! But neither as slaves nor as slaveholders!

No one in this hall—myself no more than any other— knows what feelings inspired an Egyptian sculpting a statue in the Old Kingdom; nevertheless our admiration for that statue is hardly derived from any exaltation of bourgeois values. And there's the problem exactly: to discover what it is that ensures the transcendence, the partial survival, of dead cultures.

I'm not talking about eternity; I'm talking about metamorphosis. Egypt has reappeared for us, after a disappearance of over fifteen hundred years. The metamorphosis is unforeseeable? Then we're up against a basic fact of civilization, namely the unpredictability of renaissances. But I prefer an unpredictable world to a world pretending to be what it isn't.

Europe's current drama is the death of man. With the atom bomb, and even before, we came to realize that what the nineteenth century called "progress" had extorted a heavy ransom. We realized that the world had become dualistic again, and that man's immense, unmortgaged hope for the future was no longer valid.

But it isn't because nineteenth-century optimism has disappeared that there's no more human thought! Since when has striving depended on immediate optimism? If that were true, there would have been no French Resistance before 1944. More than one old adage tells us to begin even without hope.

Man must be created again, yes, but not from sentimental cartoons. Europe is still defending the world's highest intellectual values. To know that, you need only imagine Europe dead. If, on the spot that was Florence, on the spot that was Paris, we'd come to the time when "the swaying and murmurous rushes shall bow," do you really think it would be very long before they became holy places in man's memory?

Only we Europeans have ceased to believe in Europe: in apprehensive and distant veneration the world still gazes upon these old hands groping in shadow. . . .

If Europe is thinking not in terms of liberty but in terms of destiny, it's not for the first time. Things were going pretty badly about the time of the Battle of Mohács. Things were going pretty badly when Michelangelo carved on the pedestal of "Night," "If it be to open thine eyes upon tyranny, mayest thou never waken."

So there's no question of Europe going under. I wish they'd stop that nonsense! On the one hand, there's a hypothesis: Europe is becoming a principal element of the Atlantic civilization. And on the other hand there's a question: what is Europe becoming in the Soviet view of the world? The Atlantic civilization invokes and, deep down, respects Europe as a culture; the Soviet view scorns its past, hates its present, and accepts only a European future empty of all that Europe was.

Europe's values are threatened from within by techniques developed in media that appeal to collective passions: press, movies, radio, advertising—in a word, propaganda. In a more elegant style, "psychological manipulation."

Those techniques are most highly developed in the countries we've just been talking about. In America they are primarily in the service of an economic system and tend to force the individual to buy things. In Russia they're in the service of a political system and tend to force the citizen into unquestioning loyalty to his leaders' ideology; for that, they involve the whole person.

Let's not confuse the application of such techniques in their countries of origin with their effect on Europe, especially France. The effect of American psychotechniques on our culture is secondary; that of Russia's psychotechniques means to be decisive.

And above all let's not talk tonight about some future culture, which Russian psychotechniques always refer to. Let's talk about what is: the totality of Soviet techniques in France today amounts practically to a systematic organization of lies selected for their effectiveness.

[189]

General de Gaulle is "against the Republic" (because he reestablished it?) "against the Jews" (because he abrogated the racial laws?), against France—it's instructive that just about once a week somebody can write, without being laughed at, that de Gaulle is "against France"—the one man who, during this country's terrible sleep, upheld her honor as an invincible ideal.

The interesting thing is that the Stalinists know as well as we do that all this is utterly false. It's the same method advertising uses: you put the same wrapper around soap and hope. It's always a matter of creating the conditioned reflex; that is, to make certain words and phrases, systematically grafted to certain names, link those names to the emotions habitually evoked by the words and phrases. To attribute your own faults to your opponent, so the reader becomes hopelessly confused, is another common procedure. Example: "the American party."*

Let me insist: I'm not discussing the justice or injustice of articles in *L'Humanité*, but describing the techniques that underlie the most serious psychological assault the world has seen for some centuries. On the intellectual level, to tarnish your adversary's name at the start is to render a dialogue impossible. Jean Paulhan tried for a whole year to convince the Stalinists that he'd said what he said —all in vain.

Attack on the moral level above all: in this mode of thought what you need is that your adversary be not an adversary but what the eighteenth century used to call a villain.

This propaganda strikes one note only: indignation. (That's what makes it so tiresome, by the way.) And this system, resting on the fundamental postulate that the end justifies the means—so that the end is the only morality— is

* Left-wing epithet for the Gaullists at the time. (Tr.)

the most stubbornly and constantly self-righteous system of propaganda we've ever known.

In intellectual circles this technique aims at making either allies or (in Russia) Stalinists.

About those allies:

First we have a hoary hoax, the Christian-ethical hoax. In France some of the most basic elements of Stalinism were deliberately identified with the great appeal of Christianity. But we know now what those jokes are worth.

Second is the nationalistic hoax. This one blends all Stalinist policy since the Cominform. In Western countries its object is to prevent an economic recovery that might incline those countries toward the United States and England. For that they've had to invent the "national defense of countries menaced by the Americans."

The Stalinists would like to add a great body of bourgeois recruits to their working-class sympathizers, and by that to establish a national ideology of which the Communist party would be the spearhead, so that everything would be organized not on the Russian basis and not on the basis of class struggle, but on a basis the Stalinists had experience of in the Resistance—a union of all sincerely nationalistic forces under a Communist false nose, for Moscow's benefit.

And then comes the hoax of historical perspective. I repeat: it's time to substitute the question "What *is*?" for the constant desire to explain the hidden significance, preferably historical, of what is. They've constructed a theory of socialist realism in painting—and naturally it's as defensible as any other; but what paintings have they turned out? They're not doing paintings of socialist realism; they're doing icons of Stalin in the style of Déroulède.*

* Paul Déroulède (1846–1914), French poet and politician, president of the League of Patriots, author of *Les Chants du Soldat*. (Tr.)

To condemn Bernanos* peremptorily in the name of a mythical proletariat might be defensible if we were not also compelled to admire Garaudy's edifying novels.† Ah, all those hopes betrayed, all those outrages, all those dead, only to substitute one shelf of childish sentiment for another!

And then there's the famous hoax of revolutionary continuity. As everybody knows, the gold-braided marshals are the legitimate heirs of Lenin's leather-jacketed colleagues. This has to be explained. André Gide and I were asked to go to Hitler with the petitions protesting the conviction of Dimitrov, innocent of the Reichstag fire. It was a great honor for us (not everybody was rushing to join us). And now when Dimitrov in power has the innocent Petkov hanged, who's changed? Gide and I, or Dimitrov?

In the beginning Marxism redrew the world for the sake of liberty. The emotional freedom of the individual played a huge role in Lenin's Russia. Lenin had Chagall paint frescoes for the Jewish theater in Moscow. Today Stalin heaps shame on Chagall; who's changed?

One of my books, *Man's Fate*, made an impression on quite a few Russians in its day. Eisenstein would make a movie of it, with music by Shostakovich; Meyerhold a play, with music by Prokofiev—is that a long enough honors list of death and recantation for one book? It will be explained to me that I am ignorant of the dialectic. So are prisoners at forced labor. So are the dead.

Innumerable writers have broken away: Victor Serge, Gide, Hemingway, Dos Passos, Mauriac, so many others. And the social problem had nothing whatever to do with

* Georges Bernanos, conservative Catholic novelist, playwright, and essayist. (Tr.)

† Michel Garaudy, a left-wing novelist (later repudiated by the Communist Party). (Tr.)

it. It was never understood that our "tomorrows that sing" would be that long howl rising from the Caspian to the White Sea, and that their song would be the song of convicts.

We're here on this platform tonight and we do not repudiate Spain. Let a Stalinist stand here someday and defend Trotsky!

In Russia the problem is different. It's a closed country, and by that alone cut off from the mainstream of modern culture. Now it's the country where everything has to have happened first. I quote from the young people's manual of history:

"It is a Russian schoolteacher, Sholkovsky, who developed the theory of jet propulsion. It is a Russian electrotechnician, Popov, who first invented the radio." (*Simlia Russkaia*, p. 55.)

"In capitalist countries education is a private matter and very expensive. For a very large number of young men and women it is an unattainable desire and dream." (Ibid., p. 277.)

Enough.

On the positive side, there is a mode of thought that tends to exalt solidarity, work, and a certain noble messianism, though with a note of scorn always present in liberators. But then there are psychotechniques intended to create both an image of the world and an attitude toward it that reflect most favorably on the party line. "Writers are the engineers of the soul." And how!

But for all that, they claim to have truth on their side. Let's not forget that the largest Russian newspaper is called *Pravda*: the Truth. But there are those who know better, and that raises an interesting question: in today's Russia, beginning at what rank does a man have the right to lie? Stalin knows as well as I do that public education

[193]

exists in France. There are those who are in on the game and those who aren't. And I believe that's worth thinking about; so is the contempt implied by psychological techniques. Whether it's selling soap or winning votes, there's no psychological technique that doesn't start with contempt for the buyer or the voter; otherwise it would be useless. Here the whole man is at stake; the system is a totality. The technique can exist without totalitarianism; but it follows upon totalitarianism as ineluctably as the GPU, because without police it's a vulnerable monster. For some years it was hard to deny that Trotsky built the red army: for *L'Humanité* to be fully effective, readers must be denied an opposition newspaper.

There's no free play, no give-and-take, and that's why even a small disagreement with the system leads any artist to *a recantation*.

So we come to the essential question: how can we keep psychological techniques from destroying the quality of human intelligence? There's no totalitarian art in the world anymore, if there ever was any. Christianity has no more cathedrals, but builds Sainte Clotilde, and with its portraits of Stalin, Russia scales the heights of the most conventional bourgeois art. I said "if there ever was" because the masses have never been sensitive to art as such. (On this point aristocracy and bourgeoisie are masses too.) I call artists those who are sensitive to the specific disciplines of an art; the others are sensitive to its emotional values. There is no "man who knows nothing about music"; there are those who love Mozart and those who love marches. There is no "man who knows nothing about painting"; there are those who love painting and those who love Detaille's *The Dream* or cats in baskets.* There is no "man who knows nothing about

* Edouard Detaille (1848–1912), realistic French military painter. (Tr.)

poetry"; there are those who enjoy Shakespeare and those who enjoy romantic stories. The difference between the two is that for the second group art is a means of emotional expression.

At certain periods it happens that this emotional expression blends with a very great art. That's what happened in Gothic art. The union of the deepest sentiments —love, the frailty of the human condition—and an appropriate plastic power produces an art of genius that reaches everybody. (There's something similar in the great romantic individualists: Beethoven, Wagner a little, Michelangelo surely, Rembrandt, and even Victor Hugo.)

Whether or not a certain sentimental work is artistic, it exists, it's a fact and not a theory or a principle. So the urgent problem before us is to replace the illusory appeal of whatever totalitarian culture by the genuine creation of a democratic culture. It's not a question of rubbing the masses' noses in an art they're indifferent to, but of opening the realm of culture to anyone who wants admission. In other words, the right to culture is purely and simply the desire for access to it.

[Here followed our proposed cultural program.]

So we don't make the foolish claim to be establishing a pattern for culture; we want to bring to culture some means of maintaining—in its next metamorphosis—the highest levels it has achieved for us.

We believe that the fundamental value of the European artist in our greatest ages, from the sculptors of Chartres on up to the great individualists, from Rembrandt to Victor Hugo, lies in the desire to use art and culture as objects of conquest, of mastery. More precisely, I say that genius is a difference overcome; that genius begins—

whether it's Renoir's or a Theban sculptor's—in this: a man who from his earliest years sees and studies admirable works of art that seriously distract him from the world's practicalities, one day finds himself rebelling against those forms, either because they're not serene enough for him or because they're too much so. And his need to subordinate the world, and the very works of art that have shaped him, to a truth mysterious and incommunicable except through his own work, is what determines his genius. Put another way, there is no imitative genius, there is no slavish genius. And never mind all the twaddle about the great artisans of the Middle Ages! Even in a civilization where all the artists were slaves, the imitator of forms would still be different from the slave who discovered unknown forms. In art as in other realms there is a kind of signature of genius in discovery, and that signature has been consistent throughout the five millennia of recorded history.

If there is one eternal datum of mankind, it is unquestionably the tragic ambiguity of the man who will be called, for centuries afterward, an artist—an ambiguity before a work of art that he feels more deeply than anyone, that he admires more than anyone, and that, alone of all mankind, he wants to go underground to destroy.

But if genius consists of discovery, we must also remember that the resurrection of the past is based on that discovery. At the beginning of this talk I spoke of what a renaissance might be, what a cultural heritage might be. A culture is reborn when men of genius, seeking their own truth, wrench from the depths of centuries everything that once resembled that truth, even if they aren't sure what that truth is.

The Renaissance created the ancient world at least as much as the ancient world created the Renaissance. Negro fetishes created the Fauves no more than the Fauves created Negro fetishes. And after all, the true inheritor of the art reborn in these fifty years is neither America, which collects its masterpieces, nor Russia, whose once great aspirations are now satisfied by bargain-basement icons; it's that "formalist" school of Paris, whose revivals of so many centuries seem to compose one immense family. It was our adversary Picasso who replied to *Pravda*: "I may be decadent and rotten as you say, but if you knew how to look at my painting instead of admiring all those mustachioed icons, you might notice that your pseudo-history is a small thing in the surge and swell of generations; and that my ephemeral painting happens to revive, with the Sumerian statues, a language forgotten for four thousand years."

Now: this conquest is possible only when the mind is free to roam and search. Whatever opposes the dogged impulse to discover leads, if not to the death of art (for in art there is no death; surely Egyptian art lives), then to paralysis of the artist's most fruitful faculties. We therefore proclaim the need to protect that freedom to roam and search from every tendency to determine its direction in advance. And most of all from methods of psychological manipulation based on appeals to the collective unconscious for political purposes.

First and foremost we proclaim the values not of the unconscious but of the conscious mind; not resignation but purpose, not propaganda but truth. (I know that a famous personage once asked, "What is truth?" In the area we're discussing, truth is what is verifiable.) And finally the freedom to explore. And all that not "toward what?" because we have no idea; but "starting where?" like modern science. Whether we like it or not, "The European will light his way by his own torch, even if it scorches his hand."

And we want to base these values on the present. All

[197]

reactionary thought is oriented to the past, as we've long known; all Stalinist thought centers on a Hegelianism oriented to a future impossible to verify. What we need first of all is to discover the present.

What we're defending here tonight will be defended by every great nation of the West before the end of the century. We want to recast France in the role she's played so many times, during the Romanesque and Gothic as in the nineteenth century, a role that set Europe's tone when that tone was of daring and liberty all compounded.

Intellectually speaking, you are almost all liberals. For us, the guarantee of political and intellectual freedom is not political liberalism, doomed in any confrontation with Stalinism; the guarantee of freedom is the strength of the nation at the service of ALL its citizens.

When was France great? When she did not take refuge in France. She is universalist. To the rest of the world the greatness of France is much more the cathedrals or the Revolution than Louis XIV. Some countries, like Britain —and it may be to their honor—are the greater the more alone. France has never been greater than when she spoke for all mankind, and that is why her silence is heard so poignantly today.

What will become of the human spirit? It will be what you make of it.